Esc  Through the Sacred Forest

Lich Lord Wars
Book 2

Marc Van Pelt

ISBN-13:
978-1979467261

ISBN-10:
1979467269

© 2017 by Marc Van Pelt
All rights reserved

WWW.worldofmundial.blogspot.com

Dedication
To Maddie who always brings so much laughter to my life.

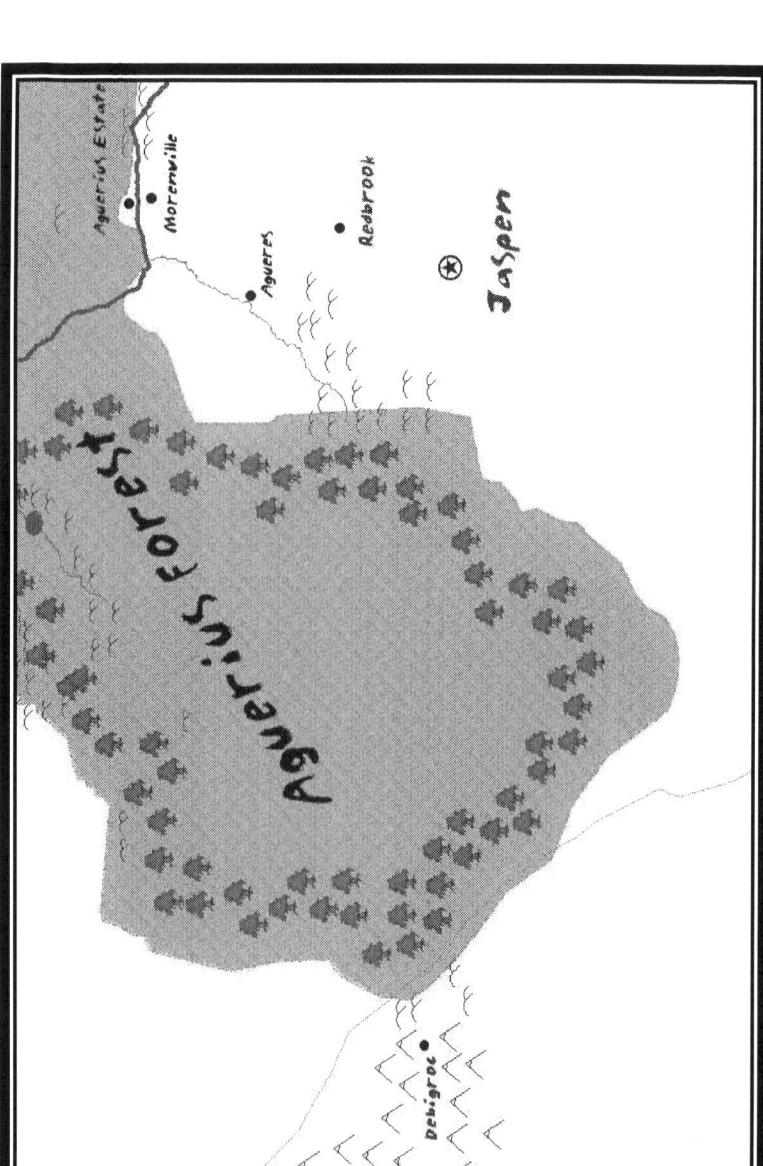

Chapter 1

"Lord Aguerius must not be allowed to take command of an army."

"He can't if he is dead. Such a small force shouldn't be that hard to wipe from the face of the land."

"Do not underestimate him or Lord Teanas. Simply delay him. First we will destroy his army, than we can worry about the more difficult tasks."

Creetan felt his stomach twist into a knot as he pulled back the arrow notched into the string of his bow. Just a week earlier archery had been nothing more than an activity. Now he found himself in a line of fellow archers; spread out and watching a force of undead revenants approaching.

He resisted the urge to once again look behind him to where his mother and siblings were taking shelter with the rest of the non-combatants -- wishing for all he was worth that he was a couple years younger and could be cowering with his siblings.

It had only been a few days since his father had returned from Demon Mountain to rescue his younger

Escape through the Sacred Forest

brother, Almas, from the Lich Lords. One of his scouts had sent word ahead of the imminent attack and, as soon as his father and brother arrived, preparation had been made for everyone in the town of Morenville and the Aguarius estate to begin their journey for the protection of the city of Jaspen, capital of the Aguarius Province.

The day before they had been joined by refugees from the towns of Redbrook and Aguares bringing the number of the company to several hundred, but with only a few dozen guards to defend them.

It was only a few minutes ago that Ulec, Almas' elvish friend, had alerted them all of the undead's impending attack. Creetan's father had only taken a few seconds to put together a defense and assigned positions to everyone trained with a weapon.

"Archers take aim!" He heard his father call out. Creetan glanced down the defense line and saw his father mounted on the back of his armored forest dragon that he used as a war mount, aiming his own bow. His father was the only archer without any guardsmen but then being a weapons master he could handle himself just fine.

Creetan's hand shook badly as he waited for the order to fire. Suddenly a calming feeling came over him; his hand stopped shaking and he found himself able to focus better.

He then noticed the harp playing faintly behind him. That would be Almas; their uncle had taught him to play, and more recently how to work magic through the playing of music. Creetan could see that the music had a similar effect on the other defenders and standing there, waiting for the order to release his arrow to begin the battle, he suddenly had a whole new appreciation for music.

"Release!" Creetan heard his father command.

Releasing his arrow he watched it shoot out with arrows from the other archers before finding its mark and causing one of the revenants to crumble to dust. Out of the corner of his eye he saw a beam of light erupt out from where his father was mounted and disintegrate a whole line of the undead attackers. His father's powers as a paladin were also useful.

Nocking another arrow he quickly shot it at one of the revenants approaching him and his guards. He took out four more before the pair of swordsmen assigned to protect him were forced to meet a group of three. Creetan continued firing at other groups of advancing creatures until he suddenly felt a wave of heat crash into him from behind. Glancing back he saw a pillar of fire rising from behind the hill where the non-combatants were taking refuge.

That would be Lord Teanas, Ulec's father, ambushing the large group of undead that were trying to sneak up on them. While Ulec could speak to animals and plants, his father had the power to control fire. It looked like he had unleashed a flaming whirlwind on the undead on the other side of the hill.

"Creetan look out!" A voice near him warned.

Turning around he found a revenant right next him moving to strike! Creetan barely dodged as he struggled to pull out his short sword. He got it out just in time to block a second strike which knocked him off balance and he fell backwards to the ground. Looking up he saw the revenant holding its sword above him ready to finish him when suddenly it began to crumble to dust. The sword dropped but a hand caught it before it could fall on him.

"Get up and pay attention to the battle before you, not the one behind."

Escape through the Sacred Forest

This was Ulec. As usual the elvish child had come from nowhere. While he looked to be no older than his twelve-year-old brother, Creetan knew the boy was over a hundred years old and had the fighting skills to go with decades of training. As was his custom he wore no shoes and even in battle he had his shoulder bag in which he kept his pet slime, named Metal.

Using the sword he had caught he took out two more nearby revenants with lightning speed before flinging the sword into a revenant that was about to kill one of Creetan's guards. A stream of acid came from his shoulder bag, into the face of yet another undead which began to instantly melt. He then pulled a knife from the sheath that another revenant was wearing as it fought Creetan's other guard. Striking the revenant he again caught a falling sword and tossed it to the first guard as he got to his feet.

Ulec then took off through the crowd of fighting men and monsters looking like a child running through a crowd at a fair, only everywhere he went revenants would start tuning to dust as he ran past them.

Embarrassed, Creetan scanned the battle nearby. The undead that had made it pass the line of defenders were being intercepted by a few warriors mounted on forest dragons, keeping them away from the women and children.

Creetan spotted two revenants pass by his guards and head his way. This time he was better prepared and had proper footing as the creatures attacked; he blocked the strike from the first one to reach him and stepped around the revenant in order to keep it between him and the second one. This allowed him to get two quick strikes in; the first one being blocked and his second finding the creature's head and reducing it to dust.

The remaining revenant attacked through the dust of its companion and Creetan felt its sword graze his leather armor as he side stepped the attack. He countered with his own sword and the creature joined the first as a pile of dust.

Scanning the battle he saw the undead creatures now pulling back.

"Warriors, hold your ground; archers, fire freely," Creetan heard his father order.

After sheathing his sword, he picked up his bow from where it had fallen and dropped three more revenants before they were out of range.

It took a few moments for him to realize that they had won and were safe. There was silence except for the sound of his brother's harp which then faded. A cheer went up from the defenders but as soon as the music stopped the fear and uncertainty Creetan had felt before the battle returned. He dropped to his knees, fighting to keep his last meal in.

"Creetan!" He heard someone call. Looking over he saw Almas running towards him and Creetan instantly had mixed emotions, embarrassment that all of the focus and ability he showed in his first battle was because of his brother's bardic abilities, and also gratitude for the fact that those abilities probably saved his life.

"Are you okay?" Almas asked as he approached and offered Creetan a hand to help him to his feet.

"I'm fine...and thanks," Creetan responded as he took his little brother's hand and stood up.

"For what? All I did was play my harp and try to help everyone focus," Almas said.

"Well it worked. I couldn't even string my arrow right, my hand was shaking so badly before you started playing," Creetan responded.

Escape through the Sacred Forest

"You still did very well for your first fight," a young voice piped up.

Creetan jumped a little at Ulec's voice. The elvish boy was standing right next to him and as Usual with Ulec, he hadn't noticed him until he spoke.

"Right, I was a half second from getting my head chopped off. One fight and I already owe my life to two children who don't even come up to my shoulders."

"At least you didn't twist your leg, almost get eaten by a forest dragon and get your life saved by a slime and a human infant." Ulec said matter-of-factly, referring to his own first life or death fight.

"Hey, I was eight, not an infant!" Almas retorted.

"To an elf, you're still an infant."

"Don't forget that this 'infant' is an inch taller than you."

Ulec gave Almas a mischievous grin but then his face grew serious as he turned towards a group of guards several hundred feet away. "Two of the guards were hurt pretty bad, I think they'll make it but they are in a lot of pain."

"Who?" Almas asked with sudden concern.

"Jestin and Torley."

"I should see if there is anything I can help with," Almas said as he hurried away.

Creetan marveled at the change in his younger brother in the past couple of weeks. Almas had barely noticed the guards around the Aguarius estate before he was kidnapped by the Lich Lords; now in just a few days he had learned each of their names and most of the names of their family members. He spent all of his time as they traveled getting to know them.

Ulec seemed to read his mind and commented, "He blames himself for the death of the two guards that were killed the day he was taken by Tornal."

The sound of Almas' harp could once again be heard coming from where the injured men were being tended to. Creetan felt all the aches and pains from the scratches and bruises he got from the battle instantly disappear.

After listening to his brother play for a moment Creetan started to say something about the deaths not being Almas' fault when a horn in the distance started to sound a series of short and long bursts.

"I never did figure out your father's code. What are they saying?" Ulec asked.

"Jaspen is under attack," Creetan answered dazed. Jaspen was the only fortified city in the area, and with undead forces attacking it, they were trapped!

Escape through the Sacred Forest

Chapter 2

"Lord Lich-El warned you not to underestimate them!"

"They will pay for this, I will go myself and personally watch the life drain from their faces!"

"Lord Lich-El's orders were..."

"Lord Lich-El isn't here! He went to deal with Jaspen. I am in command here now. We will leave immediately."

"We?"

"Yes you and some of your men. What better way to kill an Aguarius than with an Aguarius."

"We can't take our wives and children into the middle of a battle!"

"We can't leave them out here in the open either, and we have nowhere else to go; we are completely boxed in!"

High Lord Gidon Aguarius had called a quick meeting of all his men after the horns had alerted them that Jaspen was under attack. He was letting his men give their opinions as he tried to determine his own.

If it was just them, he would have led them right to Jaspen's aid but they had several towns' worth of families with them, depending on them for protection. On the other hand, they were completely exposed where they were.

"Our only option right now is to find a defensible position, dig in, and hope the siege is broken," Gidon said.

"That won't work," a young voice spoke up.

Everyone turned to the source of the voice to find Ulec sitting on the ground, with one leg extended and the other folded against his chest, right at the outskirts of the group of men. Next to him was a gray puddle happily making a meal of a revenant's sword. Almas could be seen several feet back at a more respectable distance with an uncomfortable look as he watched.

"Almas!" Gidon's second-in-command, Jarad spoke sharply, "Please take your friend and leave-"

"Its fine Jarad let him speak," Gidon interceded as he nodded to Almas to also approach; both boys while young had fought or acted bravely in battle and had earned a spot in the planning.

Ulec continued immediately, "The city's walls were breached badly a few minutes ago. The city is being overrun as we speak. The defenders are engaged in a fighting retreat towards the keep."

"They couldn't have breached the walls so quickly!" one soldier exclaimed in disbelief while another demanded to know how he knew.

Ulec's father spoke up, "My son has far reaching vision, and he was the one that alerted us to the recent attack. As far as the wall being breeched, Lich-El could easily breech those walls in moments."

Ulec nodded in confirmation, then looking at Gidon said, "Your men there are going to use the passage to evacuate everyone taking refuge in the keep."

"What passage?" Another soldier asked.

"After the fall of the Valen Province I ordered secret escape passages from all major cities and towns in this province. It should give the people a chance to flee. Sadly we don't have one here and our position is even more perilous. We are completely alone now and surrounded," Gidon answered.

"Cross the forest into the Forjad Province," Almas spoke up for the first time.

"Sorry Almas," Teanas responded immediately, "but the southern part of Aguarius Forest is strictly off limits, the forest won't tolerate trespassers here as it does in the north.

Almas looked nervously at Ulec who seemed withdrawn. After a few moments Ulec looked up to Gidon and said, "If everyone stays together and on the path provided, then they will be permitted to enter long enough to cross over to the city of Debigroc; but anyone leaving on their own, or that goes out of sight of the path, would do so under pain of death. I wouldn't be able to save them."

"Ulec, I don't think this is a good idea," Teanas cautioned his son.

"Tornal attacked the forest, as well as Almas, Seacra and me while under the forest's protection. Because we all have a common enemy, we can allow this under the conditions given," Ulec responded and looking his father in the eye said with authority, "It's my choice to make."

Almas' eyes grew wide and even Gidon raised an eyebrow. In all the years he had known Ulec, this was the closest to disrespect he had ever seen the young elf show towards his father.

"Very well," Teanas said not showing any acknowledgement to Ulec's tone.

Escape through the Sacred Forest

For the first time ever, Gidon realized that Ulec, despite his age, had supreme authority over the sacred forest. Even Teanas deferred to his son's decisions concerning it. Was it the boy's power over living things that gave him such authority? Gidon felt there was much more to this than was apparent. All these years he had known them there was still so much he didn't understand.

Suddenly Gidon realized all eyes were on him waiting for his decision. He would have to consider these things later.

"I think crossing the forest is the only choice we have. Notify the families under your care and make sure they all understand the rules Ulec gave us. We head west in twenty minutes."

"You might want to leave sooner," Ulec said looking as if he had come into himself again, "A large force of revenants and Kadus Knights just left Jaspen and I think they are headed towards us.

Chapter 3

"It seems that Lord Gidon has learned from the past."

"The people in the keep?"

"Gone. Everywhere we go the people seem to melt away. Lord Aguarius was ready, not to fight us but to run and hide."

"The coward."

"Believe that and you will deserve your fate. Where is he now?"

"Heading west; towards the border of the forest."

"Really? Than he is out of our reach for now."

"Maybe not, Ormeun has gone after him."

"Ormeun should pay better attention to his enemies. Gidon knows you never fight your enemies on their terms."

All of Gidon's experience told him to find another defensible position and fight off the pursuing undead. Right now they were just a long line of exposed people moving at the best pace the old and the young of the group could muster.

Ulec insisted that if they continued as they were that they would reach safety in time, but the woodland began to thicken as they approached the boarder of the sacred forest and he couldn't help but worry.

As Gidon helped the line of refugees move forward he found Ulec leaning against a tree watching the road weary people pass by. He had what most would describe as a sullen expression but Gidon knew the young elf well enough to know that it was the expression he had whenever his mind was elsewhere among the plants and animals.

Almas was pacing nearby showing the anxiety that his friend didn't. Gidon felt a pang of sorrow at how his second born seemed to have aged several years in the past week. The worries of a man now creasing his face. Yet he couldn't dwell on it. Right now the physical safety of his children was more important than the emotional. He could worry about healing those scars when his family was safe.

"Ulec," Gidon addressed the elvish boy, "my scouts report that the undead forces will overtake the rear of our column before they reach the border of the forest."

Ulec didn't even look up as he answered, "I know--I'm working on it."

"Working on what?"

"Slowing them down," Ulec said with a smile slowly spreading across his face. Finally looking up he added, "We were caught by surprise last time. This time the forest will be ready. The front of the column is getting close to the border, we should move up the line."

Ulec turned and walked off at a quick pace towards the front of the line of refugees. Gidon glanced at Almas who just shrugged and went to follow. Gidon couldn't help but ask himself why elves had to be so mysterious all the time.

As he moved to catch up with the boys he heard wolf howls and it was only a few moments later he caught a glimpse of a large pack of wolves running in the opposite direction of the refugees.

"Are those dire wolves?"

Gidon looked back and noticed Lamuem nearby shepherding a group of children. The ranger had taken it on himself to keep an eye on the large group of children rescued from Demon Mountain. Izybel had fitted him with a peg leg a few days ago and the ranger was already walking without crutches and as fast as any man still with both legs.

Before Gidon could respond to the man's question Almas, who had stopped to watch the wolves pass, asked, "Dire wolves?"

Nodding, Gidon answered, "Dire wolves are also called wolf lords. They are largest and smartest of all wolves. The god Mundial created animal lords to rule over the different kinds of animals. Most animal lords live in or near the sacred forests."

"They look like Crusty, just bigger."

Crusty was Almas' pet wolf that Ulec had given him to raise four years earlier. Almas had raised the wolf and it had been a constant companion to the boys along with Ulec's pet slime, Metal which the elf kept in his shoulder bag.

"That's because Crusty is a dire wolf. He's just a lot younger than those you see there. Come on, we need to catch up with Ulec."

Lemuem raised an eyebrow as they continued walking, "Your son has a pet dire wolf?"

"It's a long story, but yes, he was injured defending Almas; he went back into the forest right after we got back. I'm sure his pack in that part of the forest is taking care of him."

Escape through the Sacred Forest

Walking at a brisk pace that forced Almas to part walk, part jog to keep up with his shorter legs, they soon reached the head of the column.

Ulec was ahead of the column with Lord Teanas standing near a wall of vegetation with a tunnel-like opening. Gidon motioned to several of his men to follow him and hurried ahead to where the two elves waited by what could only be the entrance to the sacred forest. He noticed that Lemuem and his flock of children kept pace behind them.

Ulec addressed Gidon as they arrived, "My father will lead the way. This is the most sacred part of the forest so make sure that everyone understands that they cannot leave the path. If anyone moves beyond sight of the path or the group they will lose the protection granted them."

"Where will you be?" Gidon asked.

"The back of the column, the closer I am to the animals slowing down the revenants, the less strain the connection I have with them takes on me."

"I'll go with you," Gidon stated, and as Ulec nodded in agreement Gidon continued speaking before his son could ask the question he knew was coming, "Almas, you stay up here and help Lord Teanas and your mother."

Almas looked like he was about to argue but seemed to stop himself and simply nodded.

Gidon gave his son an appreciative nod before leaving with Ulec back towards the end of the column.

After walking in silence for a few minutes, Ulec spoke up, "Deleta is with the force attacking us."

Gidon sighed, he had only recently learned that his nephew was not only alive but was currently the leader of the Kadus knights. They were living people that, for whatever reason, had pledged loyalty to the lich lords.

"Is there anything you can do for him?" Gidon asked.

"I can't stop the forest from defending itself. As long as he is fighting for the Lich Lords he is in danger-- but I will do what I can."

They passed the end of the column and far sooner than Gidon was comfortable with he could hear the sounds of wolves engaged in battle.

Gidon began moving more cautiously but Ulec continued to move with complete confidence. In no time they came across the scout that had been assigned to keep sight with the enemy.

"My lord," the scout said in surprise, "They are just beyond that grove of trees! You shouldn't be this close!"

"Thank you for your concern," Gidon said, "Report."

The scout gave a quick bow and reported, "They seem to be bogged down in the shrubbery, the wolves and other animals seem to be able to move almost unimpeded which is taking a toll on the Lich's forces but they just keep cutting their way through."

Gidon nodded and turning to face Ulec began, "What would you suggest -"

Of course the elvish boy had slipped out of sight when he hadn't been looking. Gidon sighed and returned his attention back to the scout.

"Can you show them to me?"

The scout led him to a nearby mound with several trees. The spot provided both an elevated view and enough cover to let them view the approaching enemy without much risk of being spotted.

Both revenants and Kadus knights were using swords to cut through thick shrubs. Gidon caught glimpses of movement under the cover of the plants and saw both

Escape through the Sacred Forest

a revenant and a knight suddenly drop out of sight and not return.

Gidon smiled -- this was costing them, in both time and numbers.

Suddenly all the undead turned sharply to their right. Looking ahead along their path he saw Ulec's head above the top of the vegetation in the center of a group of five...wait, now four undead.

He couldn't see what Ulec was doing but within a few moments all the revenants nearby were gone and Ulec began to retreat back away from the undead and knights now converging on him.

The very fact that he could see him moving back told Gidon that Ulec was purposely drawing the enemy off.

"I think I've seen enough," Gidon said, "let's get heading back."

"Will the boy be okay?" Asked the scout with concern.

"As long as he doesn't have to worry about us, he can fade into the woods at will. Let's catch up with our people."

Almas had always thought he knew Aguarius Forest. It turns out the small portion of the forest that had been his childhood playground was the most normal part of the forest. The western leg of it was nothing like what he was familiar with.

Shortly after entering the forest it turned dark and scary. Both sides of the path were lined with brier bushes taller than Almas and the trees had almost no visible leaves.

Almas had seen Ulec make the forest look scary before, but this part was the creepiest woodland he had ever seen.

Then suddenly the forest seemed to open up and he saw another amazing sight. A grove of massive trees. They were tall with thick trunks and unbelievably thick branches. The branches stretched out and intertwined with branches and trunks of nearby trees.

Many of the intermingled branches were thick enough you could comfortably walk along them from tree to tree. In fact the path they were following led right up to one such branch that had bowed down to the ground. The branch was wide enough that even the wagons could roll right up the branch and with clusters of smaller branches lining the side of the large limb forming a kind of guardrail. Almas realized that this branch was part of the path.

He followed Lord Teanas up to where the path led onto the branch. The tip was buried so it made a perfect ramp that the wagons would have no trouble rolling onto.

Lord Teanas addressed Jarad, "Make sure everyone understands that from this point we must stay on the branches, if anyone falls off onto the ground it will be certain death."

Almas looked at the ground under the latticework of branches and noticed that just behind where the branch touched the ground that there was nothing on the forest floor. Aside from the trees, nothing grew; no plants or shrubbery. He couldn't even see so much as a fallen leaf or branch; just dead earth.

"Is there some kind of there?" asked Jarad.

"No those are firewater trees."

The speaker was Lemuem but he didn't get a chance to say any more before Lord Teanas spoke up.

Escape through the Sacred Forest

"We don't have time for further explanation. We have to get the people into the branches as quickly as possible."

With that he led the way up the branch. Jarad ordered a few men to spread warning about staying off the ground and then followed the Elf Lord. Lemuem told a few of the older children he had been taking care of to take the younger ones ahead and then he stood at the end of the branch as people and wagons began passing by up the branch.

"You're staying here?" Almas asked.

I think I know what your elf friends are planning and there is no way I'm missing this."

"What do you think they're planning?"

Lemuem flashed Almas a mysterious smirk, "Can't spoil a good surprise. Just wait here a bit.

Soon everyone had passed by except the rearguards who were just starting to insist that he and Lemuem move along after the rest when Almas saw his father, Ulec, and the remaining scouts arrive.

"They're only a few minutes behind us. Everyone hurry along," Almas' father said and then looking pointedly at his son asked, "Why are you still here?"

"That doesn't matter right now," Ulec interrupted, "Everyone on the branch."

Ulec was the last onto the branch and had everyone move several feet up the branch while he stood on the end and closed his eyes.

Almas was worrying about how Ulec seemed to be getting more pale and sickly looking with each passing hour when he felt the ground underneath him suddenly yet slowly start moving. To his astonishment he realized the branch was beginning to rise.

It was slow at first but the ground at the spot where the branch disappeared into the ground broke apart as several feet of the branch that had been buried rose at an increasing rate.

"Now that's a trick," exclaimed Lemuem as the wood cricked and cracked its way higher and higher.

Soon the branch was high above the ground and beyond reach of the approaching undead and knights. Ulec turned around and motioned everyone to move back and soon they were all above the barren ground surrounding the enormous trunk of the tree. That was where Almas' friend leaped over the side of the branch that was turned upward making a natural guardrail.

Ulec landed on a small limb jutting out of the main branch and taking a few steps out stood balancing effortlessly facing back in the direction they had come.

Almas peered over the side and asked, "What are you doing?"

"I don't like watching people die without at least giving them a warning," Ulec responded.

Escape through the Sacred Forest

Chapter 4

"They have entered the forest."
"Then they are out of our reach for now."
"The children weren't out of my reach in the forest.
"Think of the losses you suffered in the most tame and tranquil part of the forest. They have entered Mundial's most holy land. During the War of Destruction, an entire fleet of Sky Chariots were sent to the heart of the sacred forest; none returned. The same will happen to anyone and anything that enters without permission."

Almas, looking back, could now see forms approaching from amongst the vegetation. The form of Almas' father suddenly appeared right next to him partially blocking his view. A glance up revealed his father looking down at him and the High Lord said in a serious tone, "Keep your head down."

Almas nodded and then peeked around his father and watched as the first of the revenants approached the boundary of the vegetation and the barren ground.

Before any could step over the boundary Ulec called out, "That is far enough. You are commanded to proceed no further."

Escape through the Sacred Forest

Amazingly the revenants stopped. After a moment of the undead army gathering behind the first line of still revenants, Almas noticed one moving through the crowd that was different.

Even from this distance Almas could see this one didn't have the same vacant look in its eyes that the rest had. This one had intelligence in them.

The Lich Lord moved its way through the army of revenants and knights but stopped a few rows back from the front line, keeping several of its revenants between itself and the refugees in the tree.

"Who are you to command us?" The Lich bellowed out, eyeing the small elvish boy standing above it in the tree.

"I am the Guardian of the holy forest of Mundial. These people have been given sanctuary and you have been forbidden to enter," Ulec declared with surprising authority.

The Lich Lord smiled and answered, "Mundial is dead...and it will take more than you and a few animals to stop us."

"If you approach any further you will be destroyed," Ulec stated flatly and continued, "This is your last warning."

The Lich Lord said nothing. The only response was the army resumed its march into the clearing.

Almas' father leaned a little more in front of Almas and Ulec just bowed his head and shook it sadly with his eyes closed.

Almas knew that once the undead reached the trunk of the tree they would be able to march right up the huge mound that made up the base of the tree right to the huge branches they and the other refugees were perched on. He was about to ask if it was wise to just be standing there when Lemuem spoke.

"That's it for them."

"What do you mean?" Almas asked.

Lemuem gave an evil grin and answered, "Just watch."

Turning his eyes back to the approaching army and saw the front lines stopping just at the edge of archery range and some were stringing their bows while the rear of the column was just crossing onto the clearing.

Suddenly, the Lich Lord got an alarmed look on his face and turned to look towards the back of the column. Almas looked just in time to see the back row of revenants suddenly crumble into dust. He also heard a muffled cry as one of the knights disappeared from view.

The army moved forward away from whatever was taking out the back rows as the second and most of the third row vanished.

"What's going on," Almas asked with some sense of alarm. The throng of undead and humans blocking his view of the back of the army.

Lemuem answered, "Look at the ground around the base of the tree and around the edge of the clearing."

Almas did, and saw a dark shadow spreading outwards from the base of the tree and another one spreading inward from the outside edge of the clearing. As the shadow coming from the edge of the clearing reached a revenant or knight they would in moments collapse in pain or crumple to dust.

"What is that?" Almas asked.

"Those," Lemuem said, "are ants."

"Ants?" Almas asked incredulously.

"Firewater Ants," Ulec confirmed as he looked down sadly at the doomed army below, "They will strip just

Escape through the Sacred Forest

about any animal to the bones in seconds and eventually the bones themselves in about a minute."

"I think we've seen enough", Lord Aguarius said as he started to turn Almas away.

Almas knew that by "we" his father was speaking for his son, which he had seen enough; and in this case he agreed. He started to let his father turn him away when he saw something, or more accurately he saw someone below he recognized.

"Deleta!"

He was near the lich lord gathering his knights away from the advancing shadows. Meanwhile the revenants were trying to use the flats of their weapons to try to sweep a path through the ants back to the edge of the clearing, but the ant's march was too swift. Dents made in the advancing insects' line filled almost instantly in and more often than not they overtook the revenant destroying it within seconds.

"Ulec!" Almas started.

Ulec just shook his head, "There is nothing I can do. Once the ants sense something on the ground above them they come out in a frenzy. I can't control them."

Suddenly all the revenants crumbled all at the same time and Almas realized that the lich lord, having his attention on the ants approaching from the edge of the clearing had failed to notice the ones coming from the base of the tree which overtook him. With only time for a quick shout of surprise he was gone. Now only Deleta and a few of his knights remained.

Some tried to make it across the mass of ants by making long leaping steps out of the clearing but the insects were too fast and even the few moments contact with the ground was enough for the ants to attack their feet and cause them to trip in pain to be swallowed up instantly by the shadow.

Deleta watched and with only seconds left yelled something to his remaining knights that Almas couldn't make out. Then with what running start he could get in the little room he had left he leapt over the mass of ants. As he started to come down from his leap he pulled his feet up under him and slipped his shield under his feet. He landed on the shield and slid a few moments before making another great leap off the shield and landing with a roll just outside the clearing onto safe ground.

One of his knights didn't leap far enough and another lost his balance on the shield but three others made it to safety. Deleta checked on the other three survivors before looking up at Almas' group with a look of pure hatred. After a few moments wolves could be heard howling nearby and at the insistence of his men he turned and fled with them towards the boundary of the forest.

"I'll give him this," Lemuem said, "the young man is smart. Few people have ever wandered under a firewater tree and lived to tell about it."

"How do you know about them," Almas asked.

"I've seen a few," Lemuem said with a shrug.

"The Ranger's Guild built their capital city in the trees of a firewater tree forest," Ulec stated as he rejoined the group on the main branch.

Lemuem glared. "No one outside the Ranger's Guild is supposed to know that."

Ulec shrugged and said ignoring Lemuem, "We should catch up with the rest of the group. I shouldn't be too far from them.

Escape through the Sacred Forest

Chapter 5

"Congratulations on surviving your visit to the forest of death. You seem a little more subdued than normal, your first close brush with death?"

"No my lord, it's just that Ulec was with them, I had almost forgot about him. Father had just told me about him and his family right before he died. We had started to become friends, I can't believe he was with them, that he actually tried to kill me."

"Do not mistake Ulec's ability to speak to the forest as being able to control it. Do not mistake the forest's action as his. Soon they will leave the forest and you will have another chance. Clear your mind, I will have a special task for you."

"Will I like this task?"

"No my boy, I think you won't, but you are the only one I trust."

"So all these trees have millions of ants under them?" Almas asked Ulec.

All of the power Ulec had been radiating had faded and once again he seemed pale and frail--the strain on the elvish boy was obvious.

Escape through the Sacred Forest

"They need each other," Ulec answered still a little out of breath, "The tree roots provide a source of food for the infant ants and the ants bring nutrients down to the roots."

"Why do they call them firewater trees?" Cady asked. She and Giddy had been walking with the two boys since they had caught up to the main group.

"The Ranger's Guild named them that because the sap of the tree catches fire as soon as it touches the air," he answered.

"Really?" Giddy exclaimed. "Wouldn't that catch the tree on fire?"

Ulec laughed, "Not easily. The bark is fire proof."

The refugees had been following the network of branches over the nearly barren ground among the enormous firewater trees for hours now. Almas was starting to wonder if they would have to camp for the night among the branches. He had asked Ulec if that would be the case. His friend had shook his head and told him they would come out of the firewater trees a couple of hours before sunset.

So they had continued mostly in silence. The exhaustion clear on the face of almost every refugee and soldier. When they finally stepped of the branch road onto solid ground most people wanted to set camp right there. Ulec however recommended that they go just a little further so no one accidentally wondered onto the ants' harvesting ground.

When they did set camp, most ate a small meal and went right to sleep. While Ulec assured Gidon that they were safe he still set up a watch around the camp. Wanting to maintain discipline.

In the morning Ulec showed the refugees a grove just outside the camp that was full of fruit trees and berry bushes. After eating their fill they recommenced their journey.

Every time Almas thought he had seen the most beautiful part of the forest he came to a newer and even more spectacular part of it. The lushness and colors was breathtaking. Again the path they followed seemed to open before them and close behind them and the path itself was covered with soft grass that cushioned their aching feet, yet allowed the wagons to roll freely.

Everyone seemed to be traveling much easier. Everyone that was except Ulec. The elvish boy seemed paler and slower than he had before. He also seemed to be constantly out of breath. All of the Aguarius children asked him several times throughout the day if he was okay, to which he responded he was just tired.

They stopped early that day. Ulec told them there would be another firewater tree forest coming up before they left the western part of Aguarius Forest and there would be no access to water if they camped further down the path.

That night Almas was wondering among the refugees as they were finishing supper. The people sat and ate in silence. They were tired, scared, and broken despite the beauty and safety that they were, for the moment, surrounded by.

"They need something to raise their spirit," he heard Ulec's voice next to him.

Almas turned to face his best friend. "What do you suggest we do?"

"We?" Ulec asked with a raised eyebrow. "I'm not the one trained as a bard here."

Almas sighed. He wished his Uncle, an accomplished bard, was here. His friend was right, the

Escape through the Sacred Forest

people desperately needed the service of a bard. Sadly he as an apprentice bard was the best they had available.

Going back to his own family's campsite he quickly retrieved his ocarina. It and his lap harp were the only instruments they had brought with them.

"What are you doing?" Giddy asked as he started walking away with the ocarina.

"We need to get some life back into the people here. We need some music," he said.

He took a few more steps before he stopped. An idea had come to him. Turning around to face his younger brother and sister.

"Would you two like to help?"

Cady looked at him a little suspiciously. "How?"

"Remember that dance Uncle Marpel taught us last time he was here?"

"A little," Giddy answered not sounding very sure he liked where this was going.

"That's okay. I remember it and I can guide you both through the music if you let me," Almas said.

"I don't know," Cady said. "In front of everyone?"

"Look at them all," Almas said, "They need something to lift their spirits. Help them forget about our situation for a bit and remember what it's like to live. They need this."

The two children looked around and those families camping nearby. They looked at their bleak faces and with resigned looks they both nodded.

Almas found a small clearing on the edge of camp and took a couple minutes to plan out how he wanted everything to go. Once he had everything planned out in his head he began playing his ocarina.

It was a slow peaceful tune and in the music he put feelings of that peace and also hope into the music along with an invitation to come listen.

The music flowed out and the refugees responded. Some alone and some with their families or friends, but the music brought them.

After several minutes he finished the song. Seeing that most the camp was there and not seeing any more coming he turned to Cady and Giddy.

"Alright, just let the music guide you and I'll take care of the rest."

His younger siblings both nodded nervously and went and hid in some bushes out of view. Once they couldn't be seen Almas put the ocarina to his lips once more. This time he started playing a playful, mischievous song.

Giddy skipped into view and once he got to the center of the clearing switched to doing cartwheels. He then moved seamlessly into spinning with his arms stretched outward and a look of carefree childish joy on his face.

Giddy continued to dance around the clearing swinging himself from low branches on the edge of the field, jumping like a frog over rocks and being the very image of a small boy playing in the woods.

Then the tune changed to a sterner sounding tune and Giddy flipped himself over a rock and hid behind it as Cady came into view moving from spot to spot as if she was searching for some one.

Whenever she turned away from Giddy's hiding spot the boy would roll, skip, cartwheel, or flip himself with a mischievous grin to a new hiding spot. Cady continued searching always just missing catching a glimpse of her brother. At one point Giddy was behind a rock with Cady right on the other side looking for him. Almas hit a high note and magically prompted Giddy to rise at the same time Cady looked away. He then played a low note as Giddy ducked and Cady turned just missing sight of her brother. Almas alternated between the two notes as Giddy kept looking over the rock as Cady looked away and then ducking with each low note as his sister kept just missing sight of him.

This drew a laugh from the audience and Almas continued the song. He moved between the mischievous tune and the stern tune as the two children continued their antics and the crowd responding with more and more laughter and cheers. They continued with this for several minutes to the delight of the crowd.

Almas reached the last part of the song where Cady finally caught sight of Giddy and the tune changed to a faster pace to match the chase that the two siblings were enacting-- Cady trying to lay hands on her brother as Giddy dodged, rolled, and used branches to swing away from his sister all the time smiling and laughing.

The song was supposed to end with Cady getting a hold of Giddy's arm and in time with the final staccato notes pull him to face her and in the last two notes first place her free hand on one shoulder and then with her other hand release Giddy's arm and grab his other shoulder firmly capturing him on the last note.

As Almas reached the last part of the song, another idea came to him. His siblings had given almost all control to him through the magic he was putting into the music. They could resist his magical suggestions but right now they were purposely letting him control them. So as the last few notes played out, when Cady pulled Giddy to face her, Almas altered the end just a little. As Cady put her first hand on Giddy's shoulder, Giddy raised his hand up to his face and plunged his finger into his nose. Then before either child realized what was happening Almas played the final note prompting Cady to grab her brother's other shoulder and prompting Giddy to remove his finger from his nose and smearing everything he pulled out of it onto Cady's shoulder with a grin.

As he realized what he had done, a look of embarrassed horror came over Giddy's face as Cady stared at her little brother first in shock and afterwards disgust. Then seeing Giddy's expression, she figured out what happened at the same time as Giddy. They both angrily turned to face their older brother and together yelled, "Almas!"

Almas was already fleeing at his fastest sprint, and with threats and promises of what they were going to do to him they took off in pursuit.

Throughout it all the audience roared with laughter and cheered. That sound, of happy people, sounded better to Almas then any music. Definitely worth the bruises his siblings would undoubtedly inflict on him.

Chapter 6

"Where did Lich-El go?"
"He left to keep track of Lady Alixia."
"He left as we are preparing to press our attack into another province?"
"Yes, he gave us our orders, and it wouldn't be good if she returned as we are approaching victory."
"Still he has a way of vanishing right before battles."
"Would you like to trade jobs? Would you like to deal with Alixia?"
"No."
"Then go do your job."

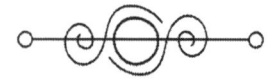

Cady couldn't sleep. There were birds chirping loudly and apparently they preferred to spend the night singing and keeping poor young refugees awake all night.

The chirping was at least pretty, but they had another day of walking ahead of them. Where was Ulec and why wasn't he telling them to be quiet? What good were elves that could talk with animals if they couldn't even get the creatures to keep the noise down?

"Almas are you awake?"

Cady was sleeping on her mat between Almas and Giddy. Almas had been having trouble sleeping since being kidnapped and then rescued from the Lich Lords. What little time he seemed to spend sleeping he was always tossing and turning and jerking awake from a nightmare he always said he couldn't remember. Oddly enough he never seemed tired despite his lack of sleep. That was why she was surprised when he didn't answer.

Sitting up she looked over at her brother. He was sleeping the most peaceably she had seen him do for days. How he, or anyone in camp for that matter, could sleep with the noise coming from the trees above was really weird.

Sure enough Giddy was also sound asleep. When no one in her family awoke when she called to them she started to get scared. Looking around the camp and saw nobody up and around.

She was about to go over to her father and try to shake him awake when she noticed movement out of the corner of her eye. Near the edge of camp walking towards the trees.

It took her a moment to figure out why that was even stranger then the apparent sleeping spell affecting the whole camp. In all the years she had known Ulec, she had never seen him arrive or leave. He always seemed to appear or disappear when no one was looking.

As he walked away she had a strange calm urge to follow him. Because it was Ulec, and she knew him, and this whole situation with the birds fit him--she got up and followed him.

She saw him leave camp and walk right next to one of the sentries. When she reached the guard she found him to be asleep while standing. She only stopped a moment to look at the odd sight before continuing after Ulec.

She entered the forest; Ulec ahead of her but still in sight. After following him for just a couple of minutes she saw Ulec stop and just stand as if waiting. She had

Escape through the Sacred Forest

covered most of the ground between them and was about to call out to him when she saw something else moving.

Cady wasn't prepared for what came out of the forest and walked up to Ulec. It was a beautiful white horse with a long horn coming out of its forehead.

She had heard of the Unicorn before. Ulec had once said it was the soul of the world; that the very life of the world was connected to the Unicorn.

And there it was right before her eyes! She cautiously approached as Ulec began to stroke her shining mane.

"She's beautiful," Cady said breathlessly.

Ulec didn't turn; he just continued to stroke the Unicorn's mane as he said, "Only a handful of mortals have ever seen her. Meeting you is one of the reasons we were allowed to enter this part of the forest."

Cady gaped at Ulec and asked in awe, "She wanted to meet me?"

"She can see, even better than me, everything that happens here in the forest. She has watched you and your brothers. She knows you are someone she can trust and has a favor to ask you."

"From me? What is it?"

"The Unicorn only appears to those she has chosen to be one of her guardians. If you're willing of course," Ulec added with a smile.

"I don't think I understand. What would she need me to do?" Cady asked.

Mostly you save people's lives by keeping them away from this forest. Also if she needs your help you will hear her voice in your mind."

"You mean I'd be like you?" Cady asked hopefully.

Ulec smiled but also shook his head, "Not quite like me. You would only be able to hear her voice. My abilities to communicate with plants and animals is something unique I was born with.

"Oh," Cady said still a little confused, "but why me?"

"Because she needs someone to trust. Who can she trust more than a paladin?"

Cady felt the look of confusion cross her face as she said, "But I'm not a paladin, my dad is the only paladin."

Ulec smiled as he said, "Yes you are. The sacred magic swirls around you even if you don't know it. You simply need to learn to use it. Trust me, you have both the heart and the power needed."

Cady looked at Ulec in astonishment. Could it be true? She had never even considered that she might have her father's gift. As far as she knew only men had been paladins. She'd have to ask her father about it.

After letting Cady be alone with her thoughts a few minutes Ulec asked, "Would you like to touch her?"

Cady looked up and saw him motion her to come closer. She timidly came forward and lightly put her fingers on the Unicorn's neck. She stroked the beautiful creature's mane for a couple of minutes with eyes full of wonder and then became somber as one more thought hit her. Facing Ulec she asked, "Why would she need me to be a guardian when she already has you?"

Ulec took a deep long breath before responding, keeping his eyes locked on the Unicorn. "I might not be able to continue as guardian for much longer and she'll need someone."

Cady faced Ulec and looked at him. He was the most pale and frail looking she had ever seen. She was afraid to ask but still did.

"Why not?"

Escape through the Sacred Forest

Ulec closed his eyes and bowed his head as he answered, "Because I'm dying."

Chapter 7

"I say we attack the moment they leave the forest."

"That wasn't Lich-El's plan. We are only to amass our army."

"Why put our trust in a traitor if we don't have to."

"Because lately those that have disobeyed him have come to bad ends. Let's wait to see where they exit the forest, then we can decide what to do."

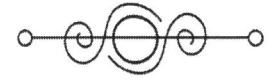

It was Gidon who had to break the news to the rest of his children the next morning. Cady was still asleep, or at least was pretending to be asleep. She was taking the news hard--just as Almas was right now.

"What do you mean he's dying? How?" Almas asked his voice rising.

Gidon took a deep breath and answered, "The weapon his shoulder was wounded with was cursed. The wound won't close or heal. The bandage he has on keeps him from bleeding to death, but it isn't stopping it from getting infected."

Creetan then asked, "Can't your healing magic do anything?"

Escape through the Sacred Forest

Gidon shook his head, "The curse blocks all healing. We have to remove the curse before I can do anything. Lady Alixia is looking for a way to do it, which is why she and Seacra left."

"So there might be a way to save him?" Creetan asked hopefully.

Gidon glanced at Almas who was quietly staring at the ground. Several emotions seemed to be fighting for control of his face.

Still watching his second born, he answered, "It's possible, but he is running out of time. I'm sure you've all noticed by now how pale and weak he seems to be growing."

Almas suddenly looked up and asked, "You said the dagger the Lich Lord cut him with was cursed right? If it was magical then it was a fieles. Shouldn't there be a fieles that can lift curses?"

"That's one if the things Lady Alixia is looking into. All we can do is wait and hope she finds something and gets back to us," Gidon answered.

Almas suddenly turned and stalked off. Gidon fought the urge to go after him knowing his son needed time alone to work through his emotions. Of all his children he knew Almas would have the hardest time with this. He hoped Lady Alixia hurried-- for the sake of both Ulec and Almas.

Almas went to the westernmost side of camp and once he was away from everyone that were busy breaking camp he called out, "I know you're out here. Come out where I can see you."

The answer came from high to his left, "You had been nearly killed and then taken prisoner by the Lich Lords. I didn't want to add to your worry."

Looking up he saw Ulec sitting on a branch a good 12 feet above the ground.

"I could still tell something was wrong, even if I didn't know what it was. And the fact you weren't telling me what it was made me worry all the more--you should have told me!"

"I'm sorry. How do you tell your best friend you're dying?"

"You're not..." Almas paused. He was about to say, 'because Lich-El ordered me to save you,' but he stopped himself.

Where did that come from? It had to be him wanting to save Ulec because they were friends. Lich-El's orders had nothing to do with anything. Almas continued, "We'll figure something out."

Ulec gave him a tired but sincere smile, "I've learned to never underestimate you. Now try not to worry too much. I have some time left. You should go get ready to leave. We have to cross another firewater tree forest today."

Almas gave his friend a long look before nodding and heading back into camp. He didn't feel comforted. Nothing felt right.

Most of the day was spent traveling among the giant branches of the firewater trees. Almas stayed by his friend's side and traveled for the most part in silence; frustrated that he couldn't think of a single way to help him.

Now many of the other refugees were starting to notice that their guide through the forest was now obviously becoming ill. So it was that the good mood granted to them the night before gave way to a more subdued mood when they came out of the firewater tree branches and set up camp just a little further past them.

Escape through the Sacred Forest

After helping set up his family's campsite, Almas found that Lord Teanas had already prepared a campfire for their family and was sitting on the ground nearby it. Ulec was also there lying on the ground asleep already, his head resting on his father's lap.

Almas tried to read Lord Teanas' stoic face but couldn't read much in it so he asked, "How is he doing?"

Lord Teanas looked over to where Almas was sitting down near the fire. He smiled warmly and answered, "He's exhausted but he's hanging on. Luckily he has his mother's strength...and her stubbornness."

"Do you think Lady Alixia will find a way to heal him?" Cady asked, also taking a spot by the fire along with the rest of the family.

"As I said she is stubborn. She won't give up until she does, and neither should we," Lord Teanas answered.

"We should wait for her. We should be trying to figure something out," Almas cut in.

"But if Father and Lord Teanas can't do anything, then what can we do?" Cady cut back.

"You would be surprised what even those as young as you can do. Kingdoms have been saved in the past by ones younger then even you," Lord Teanas added admittedly.

Cady looked at him doubtfully and asked, "How?"

Lord Teanas took a moment to consider, then smiled and started, "Many years before the War of Destruction I once traveled to the old Aguarius Province as an emissary for Mundial.

"There was an orphan boy there about Giddy's age. He was considered to be a lunatic. He saw things that weren't there and talked and played with people who didn't exist. Not simple childhood fantasies mind you; he really saw and heard them in his own mind.

"Now I was there to meet with the lord of the province and the King of Yucaipa. There was a horde of barbarians preparing to invade the kingdom and I was there to advise them.

"Sadly the horde moved quicker than we expected and launched a surprise attack. There were so many that we had no choice but to try to flee. Sadly we were overtaken and captured."

"They even captured you?" Giddy exclaimed in shock.

Lord Teanas smiled and said, "Yes, even I couldn't stand such a numerous army, but as the barbarians argued over who would take credit for capturing us, this small boy came running into the clearing where we were, screaming in terror that something was chasing him. One of the barbarians grabbed him and demanded to know what he was screaming about. The boy yelled that the king had released his screeching mind drinkers."

"Screeching mind drinkers?" Cady asked.

Creetan snorted, "And they believed the boy?"

Lord Teanas continued, "They probably wouldn't have except for the fact that as soon as he said it, the forest in the direction the boy came from suddenly filled with the sounds of screeching.

"The barbarian holding the boy was so astonished that he lost his grip on the boy, who fled the clearing screaming that they were going to drink their minds.

"Now these barbarians weren't the kind that got scared and ran. They craved glory and most drew their weapons and charged in the direction of the screeches, lusting after the glory of killing these monsters.

"Meanwhile I suddenly felt someone behind me cutting my bounds hands free. I looked behind me to find the boy moving down the line of prisoners freeing their

Escape through the Sacred Forest

handed also, all the while arguing with someone who wasn't there about the wisdom of helping us. Once we were free we quickly overpowered the few barbarians left to guard us."

"But what was making the screeching?" Almas asked.

"That is exactly what the king asked the boy. The boy answered that the mind drinkers did, as if it was obvious. It was at that moment we heard the voice of Snipies, the God if Chaos."

"You met Snipies?" Giddy asked wide-eyed.

"Many times," Lord Teanas answered, "But those are other stories. Snipies explained that the boy was using magic to make those around him experience his delusions. He further told us that the part of the boy's mind that made dreams was so strong that it made dreams even while he was awake."

"But why did Snipies appear? I thought the gods didn't appear to mortals very often," Creetan asked.

Snipies was the god of chaos; he told us the confusion the boy deliberately caused while suffering from his own confused mind had attracted him. He had come to give the boy a gift. He then handed the boy a flask of Kaynarian Blood."

Giddy interrupted again to ask what Kaynarian Blood was. His own father answered him.

"The gods who created this world called themselves Kaynarians. Their blood was said to be a source of pure magic. Giving so much magical power to a confused boy who could spread that confusion to others is something only the god of chaos would think wise."

"So what happened," Cady asked.

Lord Teanas continued, "As soon as the boy touched the flask the blood inside disappeared. With so much power, he didn't just make others see his delusions, he made all the fantasies of his mind become real."

"So the mind screechers or whatever they're called, became real?" Almas asked. Not quite believing it.

"Yes, but the barbarians made short work of them; but more than the monsters, he had in his mind an entire world that existed outside our own. We were able to pass through this world to escape the barbarians and put together an army to repel the invaders."

"He made his own world? What happened to the boy?" Giddy asked

When he touched the flask and made his fantasies real, it healed him of his confused mind as part of that. After that he could always see clearly what was real and what was not. He still had a great imagination and the ability to make his stories seem real to those that heard them. The high lord of the Aguarius Province, having no children of his own adopted him. The boy later became your ancestor, High Lord Morin Aguarius."

"Lord Morin was the boy?" Almas asked incredulously. Lord Morin was the most famous of the Aguarius line, and the first paladin. It had been his plans that had won the War of Destruction; but he had never heard any stories of his childhood before. He had never known he had spent his childhood as both a common orphan and sick in the mind.

Lord Teanas simply nodded in response to his question, while Giddy asked, "What about the world he created?

"Lord Morin and Mundial sacrificed themselves to imprison Destruction within that world, and seal him away forever; so not only did he save the kingdom while still a boy, he paved the way to save us all. So I end this story to tell you again to never think you can't make a difference simply because you are young."

Almas looked down on Ulec's sleeping form. He vowed silently to himself right there that he would find a way to save his friend. They had been through too much together to let some stupid curse take him away.

Chapter 8

"You're a fool to do this."
"We can't pass up this chance to end Lord Aguarius once and for all. I will only send my revenants and some Kadus Knights. We will never be in danger. Just do your part, Tornal, and open the way."

This would be the day they would leave the forest and entered into the Forjad Province. Giddy was excited; his grandfather Cree Forjad was the high lord in this province and he hadn't seen him since he was little. He knew his grandfather lived on the far side of the province but there was always a chance he could be visiting nearby; even in his old age.

In his excitement he didn't really notice the nervousness of those around him. They would be leaving the safety if the sacred forest and make a dash for the city of Debigroc. It was a few hours travel from where they would leave the forest; they would be on their own once again until they reached the safety of the city walls.

So as he was waiting for everyone to finish breaking camp, he was trying to find ways to amuse himself. He was looking at some rocks, looking for any he might be able to make something out of. He noticed one interesting looking stone that was roughly egg shaped with red swirls mixed into the otherwise grey stone.

He had only studied the stone for a few moments when he heard the horns signal everyone that it was time to begin the day's journey.

Slipping the stone into his pocket for future study he scurried down the forming line of refugees to where his family was standing and speaking with Lord Teanas and Ulec.

"What do you mean you're staying here?" Giddy heard Almas asking the two elves.

Ulec looked sicker than ever and had a tired voice when he answered, "I've gone as far as I can go; right now the forest is strengthening me. If I leave I won't last very long."

The line of refugees were passing by them and Giddy wondered who was leading them since his father and both the elves were still back here. He didn't see Uncle Jarad, maybe he was leading them, although he wondered how he knew where to go.

Giddy's father was speaking now gently to his brother, "Almas I know you're worried about him but this is the best place for him. He'll be safe here and won't over work himself. We on the other hand need to get going."

Almas turned to his father and asked, "Can I at least wait here with him till the end of the column passes?"

Cady piped up with a quick, "Me too?" and Gidon seemed to think a moment before his wife intervened.

"It's okay, I'll wait here with them and make sure they come."

Gidon nodded to his wife, turned and bowed to Lord Teanas and Ulec before leaving towards the front of the column.

Giddy noticed Creetan was also staying and decided to wait with his mother and siblings.

Almas again started speaking to Ulec, "So what are you going to do?"

"All I can do is wait here for my mother to find a way to lift the curse," Ulec answered with a shrug.

"What if she can't find anything in time?" Almas asked sounding a little frantic.

Ulec smiled and said reassuringly, "As long as I stay here and rest I'll hold out long enough. Don't worry."

The end of the column was passing by and the guard in charge of making sure none were left behind stood at a respectable distance waiting for them.

"Almas," his mother gently spoke, "We need to go. Say your good-byes."

Almas didn't seem to know what to say or do. Cady had no such problem, like the typical girl she was, she stepped forward and gave Ulec a big hug. The elvish boy as pale as he had been the past few days still managed to turn a shade of red and Giddy couldn't help but feel sorry for him.

She finally let him go and stood back staring at her feet and obviously trying to keep the tears in her eyes from spilling out.

Almas still stood there not seeming to know what to do. It was Ulec who stepped forward and placed his hands on top of his best friend's shoulders.

"Don't worry about me. There is nowhere safer then here and we'll find a way to get rid of this curse."

Almas looked like he was about to cry but managed to place his own hands on Ulec's shoulders and said with a nod, "Okay, you take care of yourself and we'll see you soon."

Escape through the Sacred Forest

Almas took a step back and they parted. Creetan gave Ulec a pat on his back and their mother also gave him a hug. As they started to leave Giddy, suddenly not sure what to do himself, awkwardly waved and simply said, "Bye."

Almas and Cady walked slowly. Slow enough that they were falling way behind the rest of the refugees. Mother and Creetan walked with them along with the rear guard.

They were still talking about Ulec. In fact they were so focused on their discussion that they didn't even notice passing the border of the sacred forest. One moment they were in a tunnel of dense trees and bushes and the next it was like coming out of a cave into just a normal forest.

Giddy hesitated just a moment there; in the sacred forest they had been safe and protected. Now they would be on their own, and now without Ulec or Lord Teanas.

His parents had told him it would take weeks for the undead to march around the southern tip of the forest and reach them in the Forjad Province--and that would be marching unopposed. Yet it was still scary leaving.

Tired of moving at such a slow space Giddy moved ahead to catch up with the rest of the refugees.

He had pulled a few dozen yards ahead of his slower family members when he suddenly felt his leg get hot. He stopped startled and reached into his pocket and pulled out the stone he had found earlier. It was quickly growing uncomfortably hot and he quickly dropped it to the ground and spun around when he heard a strange humming sound behind him at that same moment.

There was a pillar of light just a couple of feet from him. Taking several startled steps back away from the light he called out a frightened and drawn-out, "Mom?"

A figure emerged from the light. The pale rotted skin and spikes of bone coming out of its arms made it clear it was an undead creature.

Giddy shouted a much louder and more frantic, "Mom!" as a second form emerged from the light. He quickly backed away from the new threat as the pair of undead creatures both looked right at him.

He watched the two start to approach him as more figures emerged from the light, right before tripping over a root and falling backwards to the ground. Getting himself quickly up to a sitting position he saw the undead drawing weapons as they approached. He was about to scream for help again when he heard a loud thud as one of the creatures stumbled forward and instantly started to crumble to dust. As it crumbled he saw his mother's hatchet fall to the ground inside the growing cloud of dust. There was another softer thud as the second undead also stumbled forward with and arrow in its back.

Back at the pillar of light Giddy saw Creetan, bow in one hand and his short sword in the other, was attacking the creatures still emerging from the light. His mother ran past the combat right to Giddy and in a voice filled with worry asked, "Are you alright?"

Giddy only managed a frightened nod as his mother pulled him up. Looking back to the fighting as his mother hurriedly retrieved her hatchet, he saw his brother and the guard quickly being surrounded by the still emerging undead. Meanwhile Cady and Almas were still far beyond the light running to catch up. Suddenly Almas grabbed Cady's arm and pulled her to a stop. Giddy realized immediately why they stopped--they were cut off.

Creetan and the rearguard were being surrounded and with mother on this side of the light there was no one between them and the growing army of undead.

"Mom!" Giddy called out the warning and pointed, "Almas and Cady!"

His mother having picked up her weapon looked to where her son was pointing and seeing the situation heard his mother mutter an exclamation he never imagined his mother could say. Holding the hatchet in one hand she pulled her blacksmith hammer off her belt with her other hand and yelled over the sound if battle, "Almas! Back to the forest!"

Almas looked past the battle, locked eyes with his mother a moment, and nodded. Still clutching his sister's arm he turned and pulled her with him as he began to run. Several undead noticed them and began pursuing them.

"Giddy," his mother snapped back to him, "Go get your father!"

As she gave the order she pressed a button on the handle of both her hammer and her hatchet and both handles suddenly extended with the sound of a spring releasing.

She looked back to Giddy long enough to shout "Now!" and that was all Giddy needed. He turned and started running as fast as he could in the way he had last seen the refugees go.

He had only gone a short distance when he heard a blast from a horn behind him. Glancing back he saw the rear guard blowing his signal horn as he stood behind Creetan and his mother who were shoulder to shoulder holding off the undead as he blew a warning.

His mother was now holding what amounted to a war axe and war hammer with their extended handles. They were both slender weapons but to Giddy's astonishment his mother was cutting down undead with skill second only to his father. He had never known his mother could fight.

The sound of other horns answering the first reminded him he was supposed to be getting his father and he took off again.

He only ran about a minute when he saw several of his father's men ahead running right for him. He noticed a moment later his father wasn't far behind them.

His father had caught up to the others by the time they reached Giddy.

"What's going on?" His father demanded.

Giddy breathed out, "A light appeared and undead started coming out of it. Mother and Creetan are fighting them."

"Where's Almas and Cady?"

"They got trapped on the other side of the light. A bunch of them chased them back towards the sacred forest."

Hearing that, Giddy's father picked him up and handed him over to one of his men.

"Take him back and tell Jarad to find a defensible position and get everyone there. Every available man we can spare needs to get over here and help slow them down. Now go!"

The soldier took Giddy, flung him over his shoulders and took off back towards the refugees.

Escape through the Sacred Forest

Chapter 9

"Curse it all! Some boy moved the stone. We lost our element of surprise!"

"No time to worry about that now! Hurry and move your army through, before they have time to react!"

Almas could run faster; Cady could not. Luckily they both were smaller than the revenants chasing them. They were able to dash between trees that were to close for their undead pursuers to get through.

They made it to the border of the sacred forest but the revenants were right behind them. The whole time he was running he kept expecting the forest around them to come alive and defend them--but it stayed eerily quiet. What was Ulec doing? Surely he had noticed they were in trouble? Maybe he had fallen asleep?

The path they had used to leave the forest was even gone, which might actually be working to their advantage. While he and Cady were scampering through the thick branches and trees the revenants were having to use their swords to cut through some parts. Sadly it wasn't enough to help them lose the creatures.

Suddenly Cady grabbed his arm and pulling him to the left said, "This way!"

Escape through the Sacred Forest

Not being able to waste a moment in argument Almas followed immediately but did manage to huff out, "This isn't the way back to Ulec!"

"Trust me!" Cady responded.

Suddenly the thick foliage gave way to a clearing; in the middle of which stood a firewater tree--complete with its circle of barren ground.

Cady pulled him towards the tree and Almas looked all around for any branches bending down to the ground but he didn't see any. They would have to go around.

They got to the edge and before Almas could say anything Cady pulled him to the left and said, "This way, under that branch!"

She pulled him under a branch that extended far past the border of the barren ground but much too high for them to reach.

"We need to stay away from the blossoms," Cady said in a voice that didn't sound very sure.

Glancing up he saw blossoms sprouting from the branch several feet away.

"What's going on? How do you know?" Almas asked.

"The Unicorn told me," was all she said before they heard hacking at the edge of the clearing and saw the revenants cutting themselves out from the thick foliage. There were five of them.

Almas instantly saw that the revenants would pass under the blossoms as they approached and asked Cady, "I'm guessing we're supposed to stay right here?"

Cady gave a worried nod as the revenants came closer, weapons in hand.

"Hope this Unicorn knows what it's doing?"

"Me too," Cady agreed.

As the revenants got close to where the blossoms were Almas glanced up and to his amazement saw the flowers moving. They looked like they turning to face the approaching undead. Not only that, but the back of the flowers seemed to be swelling bigger.

Suddenly each blossom ejected a glob of liquid at the revenants and each glob seemed to instantly ignite as it shot towards the undead; turning into small fireballs that splattered flames all over the revenants quickly reducing them all to ash.

Both Almas and Cady stared as the flames began to die down. Almas broke the silence.

"I think I know why they call them fire water trees."

Cady just gave a shocked nod.

Almas finally snapped out of his shock and said, "We need to find Lord Teanas. If a whole army comes out of that magic gate then the whole province could be in danger, not just Mother and Father and the rest of the refugees."

"This way, but I can't run anymore," Cady indicated.

"Walk fast," Almas ordered and then asked, "and what's this whole 'Unicorn' thing."

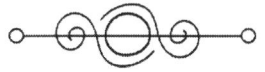

Izybel, Creetan, and his rear guard, Poxan, had broken off fighting and were fleeing with an undead army right behind them when Gidon reached them with four more of his men.

Gidon sent a wide arc of holy magic into the line of pursuing revenants. The first few rows were blasted into dust and all eight of them began a fighting retreat. He had Creetan fighting on his left and his wife on his right.

"Where are Almas and Cady?" He asked Izybel.

Escape through the Sacred Forest

"They got cut off from us. I told them to run back to the forest, a few revenants followed them. I don't know more than that," she answered nearly sobbing.

Gidon felt a sudden surge of fear and anxiety for his two young children. He inwardly cursed his current helplessness.

He could only hope Ulec and Lord Teanas would see their plight.

More of his men kept arriving, but the number of revenants seemed to be ever growing. If they didn't turn and flee soon they would be flanked shortly.

Finally one of his men came up behind him and reported, "My lord, we found a hill with only one side that is ascendable. Thick trees on that side make it a very defensible position. We have the refugees on the hill and we have the archers positioned a hundred yards back to cover your retreat."

"Our war mounts?"

"Also in position."

"Signal the retreat then." Gidon ordered

The soldier behind him immediately put a horn to his mouth and blew a signal. A moment later a barrage of arrows flew overhead as Gidon's entire line of warriors turned and fled. Everyone except Gidon.

Spreading out his arms he erected a holy shield spanning the entire line. He would only be able to hold the shield a few seconds but it would give his people a head start. As the shield began to falter he heard heavy thundering footsteps behind him.

He dropped the shield and tuned around. Behind were three forest dragons, all with heavy armor and riders. He dodged a swinging tail that flung the first line of revenants, that had surged forward, away; then he leaped up onto the dragon's back taking a seat behind the rider holding the reins and they were off. Now it was a matter of his men being faster than the revenants.

Escape through the Sacred Forest

Chapter 10

"Can you feel that?"

"Yes, magical pressure building, something immensely powerful is getting close to death, something near the battle."

"Should we pull back?"

"No, let's see what happens, it may be to our advantage."

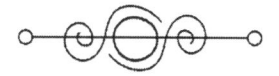

Ever since he had woken up as a prisoner of the undead, Almas had had this strange creepy feeling. It felt like death; which considering he was around or being pursued by undead all that time wasn't all that surprising.

As he and Cady neared the place they had parted with Ulec and Lord Teanas, he felt that creepy feeling suddenly intensify. It startled him and he looked back the way they came. He didn't know how but somehow he knew the feeling came from back where the undead were attacking the rest of the refugees. Something bad was happening back there. Also ahead of them the same creepy feeling seemed to be intensifying.

"What's wrong?" Cady asked with concern.

Almas glanced back the way they had come and shaking his head answered, "Just a bad feeling. We need to hurry and find Lord Teanas."

Escape through the Sacred Forest

"I think they are close," Cady said and started moving quicker, "Come on."

They found them in a small clearing. Ulec was laying on the grass. Lord Teanas was sitting next to him with his son's head on his lap letting him use it as a pillow.

"Lord Teanas!" Almas called and ran up to them.

Lord Teanas looked up startled and Almas came to an abrupt stop. Was he crying? Could an elvish lord cry?

Dread filled Almas as he looked down to his best friend. Before he could ask the question Lord Teanas answered it for him, "He's alive, just sleeping for now. Why did you come back?"

Keeping a worried eye on Ulec, Almas answered, "We were attacked by revenants just outside the sacred forest."

"What?" Lord Teanas exclaimed with a shocked expression.

Almas quickly explained what had happened. As Lord Teanas listened to his account his expression went from shocked to stricken.

Never had Almas seen so much emotion from the elf lord. He watched as Lord Teanas looked down into his son's face.

"I'll need both of you to stay here with Ulec. I need you to give him what care you can."

"He's dying now isn't he?" Almas asked.

Lord Teanas nodded, "He was sustaining himself with magic. He wanted all of you to leave with hope. Now he's fading quickly."

Lord Teanas' voice caught a little as he spoke the last few words. He took a moment to compose himself before continuing, "Please stay with him. I have to go help your family."

Lord Teanas gently moved Ulec's head from his lap and carefully laid him on the grass.

"What can we do for him?" Almas asked Lord Teanas as he quickly gathered his weapons.

"Stay with him and keep him as comfortable as you can. I'll return as soon as I can."

With one last look at his son he turned and dashed off.

Almas watched him go then looked down to his dying friend. Ulec was asleep, drenched in sweat, and the palest Almas had ever seen him.

There was also a feeling coming from Ulec that Almas couldn't quite grasp. It was similar to that creepy feeling he'd been having since being captive in the undead's base but it was like it was building up in Ulec.

Almas' mind was on this when he heard his sister asked in a frantic voice, "Isn't there something we can do?"

"I don't know," Almas answered sitting down next to his friend, "If I were paladin like Father then I could try to heal him...but if Father couldn't do it then what chance is there I could?"

Cady knelt down beside Ulec across from her brother. She tentatively put a hand on Ulec's chest and closed her eyes.

"What are you doing?" Almas asked

"Ulec told me I had the power of a paladin--I just need to learn how to use it!"

Almas just stared a few moments shocked; his sister could use paladin magic? Ulec told her? Almas felt a moment jealousy before pushing the feeling away. Cady was also Ulec's friend and now wasn't the time to dwell on negative thoughts.

Cady knelt there for a few minutes looking more and more frustrated till finally she shook her head and cried, "I can't; I just don't know how."

Almas had watched his father use healing magic and had asked him about it to know a little about how he did it. He took a moment to compose his thoughts before trying to help.

"Clear your mind and just focus on Ulec; on your connection to him. Now with that connection think of his injuries healing and try to use your heart to push those injuries to heal and his infection to fade."

Almas saw his sister's hand start to glow with a faint golden light and excitedly exclaimed, "That's it! You're doing it!"

Cady didn't respond right away. She sat concentrating a few moments before shaking her head with a troubled expression and said, "I think something's wrong. It feels like something is blocking the magic."

The glow around her hands started to fade as she began lifting her hands from Ulec's chest. Almas was about to say something along the lines of it being a good try when Ulec suddenly made a long raspy sound as he breathed out. Then there was nothing.

"Ulec?" Almas asked in alarm. Ulec's chest had stopped moving up and down and that strange feeling began to intensify even quicker. It was like the dam keeping his friends life force in him was beginning to burst.

"No, Ulec!" Almas cried beginning to shake him, "Try it again Cady! Please keep trying!"

Cady, with an expression of pure panic, put her hands back on Ulec and the glow returned. Almas stopped shaking his friend and watched intently for any reaction. The creepy feeling was so intense it was like he could almost see it...in fact, when he focused just right he could--and more.

In a moment a whole new world seemed to open up to him. He was suddenly completely aware of all the magic around him. It was as if all of his senses were focused on it. He could sense perfectly Cady's healing magic trying to enter and heal Ulec. He could also sense the curse in Ulec's shoulder snaking out a tendril and blocking her magic.

He could also sense how other magic's around him worked. There was a life force in all the living things around him. That must be the magic Ulec's sister had called Vithal that the desert elves used. Some of that magic seemed to radiate out and become another kind of magic, most likely Natela, the magic used by the elves and shadow elves. Many other kinds seemed to flow tightly around his sister, the strongest of them being her paladin magic. These must all be the magic created by humans; Trabar Magic. In dead things like fallen leaves that life force changed into yet another type of magic that Almas recognized as that source of that creepy feeling he had been having. He didn't know if this magic had a name or not; he had only heard that the Lich Lords used magic from death. This must be that very magic.

There was one more kind of magic that Almas could sense. This one came from Ulec and combined with his life force, his Vithal, made him the most powerful source of magic of all. It seemed to be contained in Ulec's blood.

Almas noticed all this in just moment but didn't have time to contemplate most of what he sensed at this time. What took all his attention was Ulec's life force--it was rapidly changing into the magic he could sense coming from things that were dead.

Escape through the Sacred Forest

He was watching his friend die. Cady was desperately trying to save him but the curse blocked every effort. He had to do something now.

Without even knowing what he was doing, as if some other force was controlling him, Almas somehow grabbed hold of the curse with his own mind and pulled hard.

The curse seemed to resist a moment before suddenly releasing its grip on Ulec and jumping right into Almas.

He gave a cry of surprise and fell backwards as intense pain exploded in his own shoulder.

Cady looked up in concern at him but before she could ask what happened Almas shouted, "Don't stop! Heal him now!"

She brought her attention back to Ulec and cried out, "It's working!"

Pushing aside the pain in his shoulder, Almas watched Cady as she healed his friend. He saw the healing magic move throughout his body wiping out infection and repairing damage. Suddenly Ulec gasped and started breathing hard and Almas saw his life-force begin returning to normal.

Both he and Cady sighed in relief and Almas told Cady to keep the healing up as long as possible.

Cady did as told but gave her brother a worried look and asked, "What happened?"

The pain in his shoulder had become a sting. Looking at it he could sense the curse there; it had transferred over to him. Looking up to his sister he simply said, "I was able to remove the curse. It didn't want to go easy."

Chapter 11

"What was that? So much death energy on the pinnacle of being released, then it was gone. Was that a god?"

"It must have been one of the elves, but I never dreamed they held so much power in them, just waiting for death to release it to us."

"Pay attention to your revenants! There is still a battle to be won."

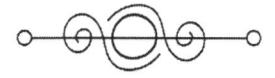

Creetan fired arrow after arrow into the gaps between trees but to little effect. The same trees that were protecting them also gave the undead protection from his arrows. He had to keep telling himself to calm down and take care to aim, he hit far more targets when he wasn't shooting arrows off in a mad panic.

He paused to survey the battle. His father was in the forefront of the battle with a short sword in each hand. The smaller weapons allowed him to fight and move easier in the close quarters of the trees. His Uncle Jarad similarly was using in a pair of hand axes right alongside his father.

Glancing along the lines he spotted a revenant knock one of the guards down. In one fluid motion he sent an arrow into the creature before it could finish the man off. He hadn't even thought about what to do, his training

Escape through the Sacred Forest

had acted before he had had a chance to second guess or worry about it. He called out to a nearby guard to go assist the man and once he was back on his feet Creetan began scanning the front line for more targets. He was still terrified but maybe if he tried to clear his mind of worries and let his training take over, he might just survive this.

Yet that chance seemed to be fading. The men were being overwhelmed. More and more he was seeing revenants about to overcome a man and it was a matter of time before he would be too late to save him with a well-placed arrow. So it was to his utter astonishment when all the revenants simultaneously began withdrawing with the Kadus knights following their lead.

"What's going on?" Creetan called to his father.

"Not sure," his father answered and addressing all the men, "Keep alert!"

After a few moments later someone called out, "Look! Smoke!"

Scanning high above the trees Creetan saw a plume of smoke rising out beyond the undead's lines.

"Could it be Lord Teanas?" Creetan called over.

Gidon studied the smoke for a moment before nodding and stating, "It's possible that Almas and Cady found him. You and your mother said they fled that way."

Addressing all his men he continued, "See to the wounded. Archers keep a lookout.

Gidon began moving up and down the line healing and repositioning men as needed. Creetan watched the forest, knowing their enemy would return.

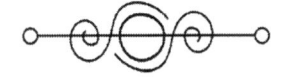

Lord Teanas had hoped to find the portal or possibly some lich lords before he was spotted but it was not to be. The undead must have feared he would appear for there were many undead scouts watching the border of the forest. Once he was spotted he fell upon the army of undead with a fury as deep as his anguish.

Within moments he was the center of a growing firestorm. He plunged himself into first the scouts and then both the regular revenants and the Kadus knights that came to face him. At first none could even approach him without being consumed in flames, but eventually the flames died down and he had to contend with his foes one on one.

Even as the enemy surrounded him he fought without thought of his own welfare. His son was dying and he intended the undead to pay dearly for all they had done. They would learn that while Lord Teanas was slow to anger, woe unto those that finally kindled the fires of his rage.

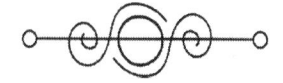

Almas watched Ulec as he rested. His shoulder was hurting more but he pushed the pain away. He studied the magic as it flowed around and from Ulec; he even saw the moment when his friend awakened.

He watched as his friend cast a spell over himself when he woke up and at first seemed to heal himself. It took him a moment to realize he didn't actually heal himself but changed himself. He changed his form from his injured self to his uninjured self like his mother and sister changed forms from their normal elvish selves to animals.

Escape through the Sacred Forest

Ulec did this before he even showed any sign that he had awaken.

"How are you feeling?" Almas asked.

Ulec's eyes snapped open and he looked at Almas with a curious look, before answering, "Better; what...happened?"

Cady answered excitedly before Almas could say anything, "You stopped breathing but Almas removed the curse and I healed you.

Ulec got up on his elbows and asked confused, "Removed? How did you remove it?"

Almas answered honestly, "I'm not completely sure. I was watching Cady trying to heal you and suddenly I could feel all the magic around me; it was almost like I could see it.

"I could see the curse on your arm blocking Cady's healing power. Without thinking I tried grabbing the curse with magic and pull it away from you. It worked--I removed the curse and Cady healed you as much as she could."

Ulec stared a moment at his best friend. "You can see, or feel magic and curses? How well?"

I can feel any kind of magic I think. Along with the curse I seem to be able to sense magic abilities like Cady's paladin abilities and the one you are using now to hide how hurt you still are.

"I think I can see all the different types of magic, including the one you're using that you never told us about. You have Kaynarian blood in you don't you?"

Now Ulec stared open mouthed at Almas. He sat there several moments before saying, "That cannot be known."

"Why didn't you tell us? Why can't anyone know?" Almas asked feeling a little bit hurt.

"The Kaynarian blood came from my real father, and it was his blood that was used to make the blood seal that imprisoned Destruction. If anyone knew who my real father was then my blood could be used to release the seal."

"That would mean your real father was Mundial!" Cady exclaimed.

"I can't believe I didn't see this before. You talk to plants and animals...the creations of Mundial," Almas murmured.

"Lord Teanas is the only father I've ever known. Wait...where is my father," Ulec perked up suddenly concerned.

Almas felt Ulec's ability to communicate with animals come alive and he could feel Ulec spreading his awareness throughout the forest.

"We were attacked outside the forest. Cady and I were forced to come back here and Lord Teanas left to go help the rest of the refugees," Almas explained.

Ulec said nothing; he was focused on what he was doing with his magic. Suddenly Almas could feel Ulec's magic use seem to focus and Ulec's expression of staring at seemingly nothing narrow.

After a moment Ulec said, "They're in trouble. They found a defendable hilltop but the undead army is huge."

"So what do we do?" Cady asked tears coming to her eyes.

Ulec seemed to start scanning the area with magic again. Almas was amazed on what his newfound ability seemed to tell him. He was even more amazed he had never noticed any sign before that he even had it.

"We send some help," Ulec answered Cady with a smile.

Escape through the Sacred Forest

Chapter 12

Focus on Lord Teanas, if killing him can generate as much death magic as we just felt, killing him could win this battle."

Teanas knew he was out of time. He had used up all the magic in the area that he could use. Now he only had enough to change the form of Mimic, his magic ring, to whatever weapon he needed.

He had burned and cut his way to within sight of where Lord Gidon and the other refugees had fortified themselves.

The undead army seemed to have halted their attack on the humans and were focusing the whole might of their army on him.

He was striking down multiple enemies with each swing and evading blows with each step. Exhaustion would cause him to make the mistake that would end his life at any moment; which came when he moved just an instant too slow and took a deep cut to his leg.

He fell to his knees and with Mimic taking the form of a halberd he swung it in a circle around him cutting all enemies within its range in half. Teanas knew that would be his last action. He would be overwhelmed in an instant and soon be with his son in the next world.

Escape through the Sacred Forest

"I failed you and your son my Lord Mundial," would be his last words

Yet the killing blow never came. It was replaced by and enormous crash all around him. Three trees had fallen practically on top of him crushing all enemies around him and creating a wall of tangled branches around him. For a short moment he was safe.

"Ulec?" Teanas whispered.

In answer a songbird landed on a branch in front of him and chirped Ulec's signal that he was alright. A sob of relief erupted from Teanas as he stood hardly noticing the pain from the gash in his leg.

He didn't know how but his son was alive; not just alive but he was okay now. The forest was coming alive now as large wolves, bears, and elk charged from the forest. Big cats sprang from trees and birds of every sort dived from the sky.

Teanas, feeling a surge of energy, sprang over the wall of branches and began cutting through the undead ranks again.

With the help of Mundial's creations, the plants and animals heeding the call of Mundial's heir, Teanas made quick progress towards the hill where Gidon's people were taking refuge.

Suddenly a large group of revenants preparing to meet him disappeared in a flash of golden light. He looked ahead and saw Lord Gidon riding his dragon mount towards him, swinging a halberd at any enemy that dared come to close.

"Get on!" Lord Gidon called as he rode up to him.

Teanas grasped the arm being extend to him and swung himself behind his human friend.

Gidon told Teanas to hold on as he turned his mount back towards the hill, the dragon's tail swinging out and smashing a group of revenants to the ground as it turned. The undead were forming line to block them but with a swing of his weapon a golden arc of light flew from the paladin's halberd destroying them at contact. They rode past the remains of the enemy and quickly made it to friendly lines.

Both Teanas and Lord Gidon leapt from the dragon mount and Gidon issued several orders to his men to ready them for an attack before turning his attention to Teanas.

"Almas and Cady?" Gidon said with a hopeful questioning tone.

"Both made it to me safely. I left them inside the borders of the forest with Ulec," Teanas answered as he knelt down from exhaustion and pain.

Lord Gidon knelt beside and placed a hand over the wound on Teanas' thigh; his hand emitting a gold light as he began to heal him.

"I wouldn't have thought Ulec still had the strength to do all this," Lord Gidon stated.

"Something must have happened. Ulec was unconscious and minutes if not moments from death when I left them. He sent a message that he's fine. I don't know what to make of it."

"What I make out," Lord Gidon said with a smile, "Is we just might make it out of this now."

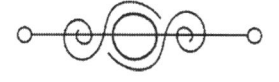

Izybel tried to watch through the dense trees with an ever growing sense of foreboding as the undead army regrouped and prepared to attack once more.

Escape through the Sacred Forest

She sat atop her husband's forest dragon mount, which had just been brought to her. With her were the few other mounted warriors, the dragons and horses not being very effective in the dense trees, along with those who were too injured for the front line.

They were to be the last line of defense for the non-combatants. She glanced back and took in once again the terrified group of children, elderly, and women tending the young; they had each been armed, everyone that could pick up and use a weapon.

Her own son, Giddy, sat on the ground with a group of children. He sat with his legs crossed holding the hilt of a short sword nervously on his lap. Izybel swore to herself he would never need to use it.

Her attention snapped back to the front line when she heard someone call out a warning that they were coming.

She couldn't see much through the trees but she saw the archers in sight begin pulling arrows back on their bows and releasing. Also see saw flashes through the trees that could only be her husband attacking with his paladin magic.

Soon the sound of metal striking metal filled her ears; as did the sound of branches falling and various animals locked in combat. "Keep alert," she ordered all those around her.

"With Lord Teanas here we might have a chance."

Izybel looked down and to the right and saw that Lemuem had approached her and had spoken. He continued, "The enemy is looking for weak points in the line. That elf is able to move quickly enough to reinforce any points the find before they can take advantage."

From what she could see it seemed to be true. The line was holding.

"I assume your tracking everything out there?" Izybel asked Lemuem.

The ranger smiled a mischievous grin at her and answered, "Only those on our side. I can't track anything I haven't been close enough to..."

Lemuem's voice trailed off as his attention returned to the battle.

"We might have a problem. We have a gap appearing on both the left and right sides of the line. The elf is moving to reinforce the right side. I think they might breach on the left."

Izybel signaled to the other defenders to be ready. Lemuem pulled out two daggers and said, "Here they come!"

Revenants began to pour out of the trees on the left side of the tree line. Izybel pulled her blacksmith hammer and hatchet and pushing a button on their thick handles, extended them into an elegant war hammer and war axe.

"Mounted warriors with me. Rest hold the line here," she ordered before commanding her mount to charge at the growing group of undead rushing towards them.

Her forest dragon ran into the enemy at full gallop, smashing revenants under its feet and picking up and crushing others in its jaws. Meanwhile Izybel's hammer and axe took out more on either side of the charging beast.

Eventually her mount slowed to a stop and the other mounted warriors formed up on either side of her to protect her flank. Now the battle became a flurry of snapping jaws, slashing claws, and flashing weapons.

Soon the flow of enemies emerging from the trees slowed and stopped as the warriors on the front line managed to close the hole in their line. As the number of enemies shrank Izybel risked a glance behind her, where she saw the few revenants that had made it past the mounted warriors were being cut down by the few guards on foot charged with protecting the refugees.

"Form up and get ready for the next wave," she ordered.

Chapter 13

"This last wave should do it. They are tired, hurt, and running out of arrows."

"Hurry, I won't be satisfied till Lord Aguarius is dead at my feet. And we've nearly exhausted our supply of death magic. Between that cursed elf and that paladin we aren't getting enough kills to replace what we are using."

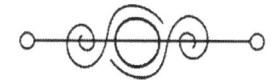

"I'm telling you I heard battle horns. They were faint but I know what I heard."

If the scout giving the report hadn't been one of his most reliable, Lord Mason would have dismissed the report out of hand. The thought of Aguarius soldiers fighting nearby was disturbing.

Word of the undead invasion had only just made it around the south leg of Aguarius forest and up to Debigroc the day before. How could any fighting have reached them so soon?

Lord Mason was lord of the city of Debigroc and tasked with guarding the north pass into the Forjad Province. Last he had heard the undead were moving southwest across the Aguarius Province and he had assumed they would enter Forjad through the south pass.

Escape through the Sacred Forest

He also thought he had at least a few weeks before the made it this far.

If the scout was right, then the war had already arrived; and from the east of all places, appearing out of nowhere as if from the forest itself. Was it possible?

Lord Mason wasted no time sending messengers to Debigroc to alert the city and began organizing scouts to go find out what was going on. He had been out with a group of his men on a training exercise but it looked like they might get some real action.

He was about to dismiss his scouts when he heard the howl. All activity in the camp suddenly stopped. It had been a dire wolf howl, but the loudest and deepest he had ever heard.

"Weapons ready," he ordered drawing his own sword.

Watching the tree-line at the edge of the field where they were camped, in the direction the howl had come, he was shocked to see the largest dire wolf he had ever seen come bounding from the trees. The beast was larger than even the largest bear he had ever seen.

Before he could give any orders the wolf slowed its pace to a trot and stopped just out of the range of the archers who were already notching arrows and taking aim.

It was when the wolf laid down and lowered its head that Lord Mason realized the wolf wasn't alone--it had passengers. Three children had been riding on the wolf's back--on the back of a huge dire wolf! It was unthinkable!

Two of the children, a boy and a girl, slid off the beast's back and began running towards him and his men. Lord Mason ordered his men to hold their fire and watched in fascinated awe as they approached him.

The pair stepped up to him and the boy held up the crest that hung around his neck. He spoke in a voice of authority beyond his apparent years.

"I'm Almas Aguarius and this is my sister, Cady. We are children of High Lord Gidon Aguarius and Lady Izybel Forjad. Our family along with refugees from the Aguarius Province are under attack by forces of the Lich Lords and we request your aid on behalf of our parents."

Lord Mason stared in stunned silence at the siblings. The crests and the obvious family resemblance supported their claim. He could do nothing but accept that these two children were High Lord Forjad's grandchildren and accept that the enemy had already made it to the borders of his land.

He looked back to the third child still sitting astride the huge wolf. There was something about the boy that didn't seem quite...human. Something about the way he held himself and something about those ears.

"Who is he," Lord Mason asked indicating to the third child.

"A friend and ally to the House Aguarius," Lord Forjad's grandson answered simply.

Lord Mason didn't need to think long on it. Only one thing mattered. His Lord's daughter and remaining grandchildren were in danger and there was only one thing he could do.

"I verify the children's crests are true. Lady Izybel and her children need us! Ready the mounts and war wagons! We leave immediately!"

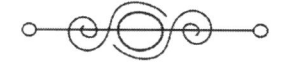

Escape through the Sacred Forest

Gidon's men were getting tired and the enemy's numbers only seemed to increase with each wave. In the last wave he had lost two men and had it not been for Lord Teanas' quick arrival the enemy would have completely broken and overwhelmed the line. As it was, he hoped that Izybel and the rear guard could manage the enemies that had slipped past them.

He didn't even want to think about the number of forest animals that had been slain in coming to their aid.

With a swing of his sword he sent an arc of holy magic into the latest wave of undead turning several rows of revenants into dust. But more were coming. As a sword thrust came at him from the side he stepped back putting a tree between himself and the undead creature attacking him. Twirling around the tree he cut down his attacker from behind.

Seeing one of his men get knocked down he extended his hand and a golden glowing bubble appeared around the guard protecting him as he quickly picked up his dropped weapon and regained his footing. The bubble disappeared as Gidon was forced to contend with the next line of revenants attacking him.

As he fought he realized this could be the wave that broke them. There seemed to be no end to them. He bashed with his shield, kicked with his feet, and his sword glowed with holy power as it cut through enemies and sent deadly bolts of magic into the endless lines of undead.

He was about to lose all hope when he heard the horns. Not the ones that had been sounding from his own ranks calling for aid whenever a moment could be spared from combat to sound them but answering horns. Aid was coming!

Both he and those who heard and understood the meaning of the approaching horns began to fight with a renewed vigor! They just had to hold on a little longer!

The enemy also heard the horns and they now knew they were quickly running out of time. They now surged forward to end it before the new threat to them arrived.

As the fighting intensified he heard another answering call coming from the same direction as the horns. The deepest loudest howl he had ever heard sounded from the depths of the forest. It was joined by howls from all of the wolves that had been fighting with them and by many more packs from all over the forest.

Even the forces of the lich lords seemed to hesitate a moment.

From the forest on the enemy's left flank came a pack of the largest wolves Gidon had ever seen. And standing impossibly on the back of the largest stood Ulec, armed with a bow.

The pack plowed into the undead army's flank with a flurry of snapping jaws. Ulec, somehow maintaining a standing position on top of the leaping wolf, fired arrow after arrow into the undead army.

Gidon saw Ulec leap to a low branch as the monstrous wolf he was riding stopped to bite a revenant cleanly in half. Ulec ran down the branch shooting arrows down into revenants before dropping to the ground to stand back to back with his father.

"Look out!"

Gidon heard the warning as he caught movement in the corner of his eye. A revenant was striking down at him but before he could react the blow was deflected by a short sword.

Escape through the Sacred Forest

He used his own sword to cut down the creature and glanced just long enough to recognize his oldest son standing next to him. He didn't even have time to thank him as the undead army was now attacking with renewed effort. Following the example of the two elves he turned his back to that of his son's and back to back they settled into the task of staying alive till help arrived.

The horns sounded again after several long minutes of intense fighting followed by the sound of falling trees. Gidon swung his sword unleashing an arc of magic clearing out all nearby enemies; giving Gidon a moment to see what was, in that moment, a truly beautiful sight.

Smashing through the trees were several huge beasts. They were huge creatures with thick brown fur and long tusks coming from the sides of their mouths underneath a very long nose; but these weren't beasts of the forest for these beasts wore armor over much of their body and carried baskets on their backs which in each sat a man holding reigns and three archers. Being pulled by each beast was a long war wagon that was basically a long box on wheels with archer slits in the side.

"Mammoth Riders," Gidon exclaimed in awe as a line of mammoths began stomping through the undead army, crushing them under tree trunk sized legs and raining arrows down on the enemy from both the baskets and the war wagons.

Gidon turned his attention back to the work of destruction on all enemies that approached him. He fought with a renewed vigor as several mammoths broke off from the others that were plowing long lines of destruction through the enemy masses and created a line of mammoths and war wagons right in front of Gidon's defensive line.

Once they had made a wall between the main mass of undead and Gidon's men, the back of the wagons dropped and armed soldiers poured and created a new defensive line.

It was as the soldiers first started pouring out that Gidon noticed the harp music coming from one of the baskets and smiled as he recognized the music being played and the strengthening effect it was having. He was now pretty sure he knew who to thank for bringing the reinforcements.

He couldn't see his second born son for he was sitting low in the basket but he was relieved to know Almas was there and unharmed enough to be using his bard skills.

As he and his men finished the few remaining enemies trapped between the two human lines he gave orders up and down his lines for those not wounded to go retrieve the refugees and get them and the wounded into the war wagons.

A man wearing the uniform of a Forjad officer approached Gidon and asked brusquely, "Where is Lady Izybel?"

"Helping to defend the refugees. She will be down with them shortly."

"I'm here now," came a voice from behind. Gidon looked behind him to see his wife riding up on Kitty, his war mount, with Giddy seated also on the mount in front of her.

The man bowed and said, "My lady, I am Lord Mason of Debigroc. We must leave. I do not believe my men will be able to hold off an onslaught like this for long."

"You will hold it until we have gotten all refugees safety in the wagons," Izybel responded.

Gidon stood silent. Now that they were in the Forjad Province, his wife was the highest authority present and he admired how easily she slipped into that role.

Escape through the Sacred Forest

"Is Cady with you also?" Izybel asked allowing only a trace of the worry he knew she felt enter her voice. Almas could still be heard playing music from the top of the mammoth lending strength and alertness to those holding the line.

"Yes, both of your children insisted on coming and using their talents to aid in your rescue. Your daughter is in this wagon here."

Lord Mason motioned them to follow him into the back of the nearest war wagon which was filling quickly with refugees. He stopped short in utter shock when he caught sight of his daughter kneeling next to an injured soldier, holding glowing hands to the man's chest. She was using holy magic to help heal the man. When had she started doing that and how did he miss the fact she had learned to use paladin skills? Izybel had also stopped abruptly in surprise.

"That's the last of the refugees my lord!" A soldier called from outside.

"Signal the war mammoths to cover us as we retrieve our men and get out of here," Lord Mason called back.

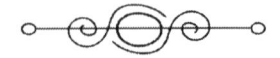

The other soldiers in the basket made sure Almas kept his head down low in the basket, so he didn't get to see the fighting; which was okay with him. His focus was on using his music to send as much power to those fighting as he could with his Bard skills and now with his new found ability to feel magic he could see it flowing from him to his instrument and from there to all the soldiers from Debigroc. He also focused and trying to ignore the pain from his shoulder where the curse that had jumped to him from Ulec had taken hold. It was beginning to sting.

Suddenly one of the men in the basket called to the others, "That's the signal! The refugees are in the wagons. Flame barrier now!"

The archers put down their bows and picked up jars that had been stacked at their feet and began to throw them over the side. With everyone's attention away from him, Almas snuck a quick glance over the side of the basket. The jars the men were throwing were breaking and bursting into flames creating a wall of flame between the undead army and the line of soldiers who were beginning to scurry into the war wagons. Meanwhile the war mammoths were stomping through the ranks of Kadus knights and revenants near the fires aiding further to the recovery of the last of the foot soldiers.

He was suddenly pushed back down by the nearest archer who told him stay down using words that men rarely used around children of high lords.

He heard someone yell, "That's it! Go!"

The mammoth lurched forward as the men continued to rain down arrows and those fire jars on the enemy as they dashed away.

After what felt like a long time but was probably only a minute or two one of the soldiers called on the other men to hold their fire. Another said in an awed voice, "Look at that..."

Almas peeked again and looked behind them. At the rear of the last war wagon trees were falling to the ground creating a tangle of branches, many in flames, keeping the undead from pursuing them.

It had to be Ulec. It was clear the soldiers had never seen anything like it. They had made it. They were safe for the moment.

Escape through the Sacred Forest

Suddenly he felt someone grab his arm.

"You're hurt!"

It was the soldier that had been in charge. He was pointing to a wet red spot on the sleeve his shirt right over were the curse was.

"I...I cut it in the forest earlier," Almas lied.

"We need to get a bandage on that," the man said.

"I'll take care of it."

Everyone whirled around to find Ulec standing in the basket folding a strip of cloth.

"How...when did you get up here?" The man asked.

Almas laughed, "I've been asking him that for years, I wouldn't expect much of an answer. He can help me with my arm."

The man shrugged and releasing Almas went to his spot in the basket and began scanning the land around them for threats along with the rest of the men in the basket.

Ulec knelt down beside Almas and pulled up his sleeve. A cut was forming on his arm. Ulec looked at it a moment before beginning to bandage it. As he worked he leaned close to Almas and said in a low voice that only Almas could hear, "That is my wound on your arm. How did you move my curse to you?"

"I'm not sure," Almas whispered back, "I just couldn't let you die."

"Better me then you," Ulec murmured.

"Not in my opinion. We have more time to figure this out now. Neither of us are dead yet."

Epilogue

"This man is as slippery as an eel."

"So after all of that you will use Lord Lich-El's plan after all?"

"Yes, provided they haven't discovered our spy."

"If they have it's your fault for acting outside of Lord Lich-El's orders.

"Remember your place human, just because you're favored by our leader, don't think you are beyond my reach."

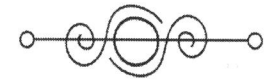

Gidon was riding in a basket atop a mammoth when they came into view of Debigroc. First there was the cliff rising high above the ground marking the beginning of the Barrier Mountains. It was a wall of stone that ran as far as could be seen to the north and the south.

They were riding towards a crack in the cliff with a manmade wall stretching the length of the crack. Gidon knew the wall was large but in comparison with the immense cliff on either side it looked tiny.

"How could such a thing come to be?" Gidon asked in awe to no one in particular.

"Mundial told me when he first found this world it was frozen. He told me this cliff was made by a mountain of ice much larger then these mountains. It carved the cliffs by sliding slowly south from the Dividing Mountains," Lord Teanas said from next to Gidon.

The high lord turned to his elvish companion, "If memory serves me Debigroc was once an elvish city?"

"It was one of our royal cities. I used to play alongside this very river with my siblings as a child."

Lord Teanas had a wistful faraway look in his eyes as he looked at the city.

"You elves built it well," Lord Mason said from behind them, "The Crafters Guild have a very high standard for their buildings and cities. We kept all the original buildings and have only added onto what was already here."

"The walls are enchanted also, "Lord Teanas added," Even Lich-El could not break through them."

"That is well, "Gidon said, "Our people can get some rest here and maybe we can see if we can't stop reacting in this war and start acting. By now the Aguarius Province should be completely evacuated and the first phase of our plan completed. Now it's time to start the second phase and show our enemies we can do more than run."

Also by Marc Van Pelt

Mathen's Flight
Fate's Foe Series Book 1

Mathen is a successful businessman thanks in no small part to a magical crest he wears around his neck that gives him glimpses into the future. His life is turned upside down when one of these glimpses shows him someone destined to become the worst and most evil tyrant the world will ever know, and shows him this person in the form of a small 8-year-old boy who just attempted to pick his pocket.

Now Mathen must face the most difficult decisions of his life. Decisions that hold the life of millions of people and the very world itself in the balance. As he makes his choices he must deal with slave traders, magical beings and a living forest that all seem to have their own interest in the boy.

Escape through the Sacred Forest

Mathen didn't go to the City of Aguares to have his life completely turned upside down. He also hadn't planned on turning the town its-self upside down. He had traveled just over a week from the City of Valen for only one thing...Rocks.

Well, stone might be a better word for it. Mathen owned more than a small number of factories that made the best stone products in all the Necromian Kingdom. He had heard of a new stone quarry outside of Aguares with unusually high quality of stone.

So it was purely with the intent of a business deal that he found himself driving his wagon through a forest of dead trees just outside Aguares in the Yucaipan Republic. It was the 3rd such forest he and his two escorts had passed through and Mathen found himself reflecting on the changes he had seen in the world during his life. It was during the course of these reflections that a voice came to his mind.

You should've seen this world in the day I was created. Only the most ancient elves can even imagine the life and beauty this land once enjoyed.

Mathen's hand moved to his chest and felt the shape of an ancient crest that hung from his neck under his shirt. The crest had been in his family for over 800 years but it wasn't the age that gave it its value. It was the soul locked away inside of it by ancient elvish magic. It was a fieles, which was the name given to living objects.

I'd rather not, Mathen thought back. *Just the decay in my own time is enough to make me sad. I'm not sure I can bear what could've been.*

The Voice responded, *you think it's hard for you? Think how some of the more ancient of the elves feel about it. In the last 800 years they have watched humans build more and more machines that aren't very friendly to nature. Just those steam engine things you guys came up with a few years ago do tend to make the air very dirty. It's no wonder they blame you guys for the decay.*

Mathen replied, *but we know humans aren't to blame. This decay started over a thousand years ago. All we can do is make best of the time the world has left and there is still quite a bit of time left.*

Much time for you perhaps, but a blink for me. And then I'll be here long after the world dies. That's my future, came the response.

It was an old argument. Mathen determined to make the best of his life and the life of others while the fieles around his neck spoke of the good ol' days and complained about the present, and the future, or lack thereof.

The fieles was named Seer. Its power was to give glimpses of the future, sometimes things that would be and at times things that might be. The glimpses would come randomly, sometimes as clear visions, or at times as vague premonitions.

Despite their arguments and different opinions the two were good friends and had developed a relationship of trust. Seer had been extremely helpful in all of Mathen's business dealings and it was on the fieles recommendation that he was now entering Aguares.

The city had spent most of the last two thousand years as a farming community. So while it was one of the largest cities in the region it was spread out and seemed very small when compared to the cities of the neighboring kingdoms and nations.

Making the city feel smaller yet was the fact the fields had lost their fertility over the last five years. Most of the population had left and only the fates knew what the rest had done to survive since the stone quarry had opened only a few months ago.

As his wagon slowly made its way down the main street towards the center of town he was amazed on how few people there were. There were a couple of sullen looking children sitting in front of a shop. A man dressed in rags lying on the side of the street in what appeared to be a drunken slumber. Mathen noticed his escorts kept resting their hands on the holsters of their firearms as they moved through the city.

I've seen cities a day after being pillaged and razed with happier and more numerous people, Seer commented.

Mathen responded, *most left when the farms failed. Those that remain are spread out. What I wonder is how they have survived these last five years with no visible source of income.*

Independently wealthy? Seer asked.

You can answer that better than me. I've been here once before and that was 40 years ago. You've been here, what, a couple dozen times in the last 500 years? Mathen shot back.

Thirty-eight. And you're right. This place should've been completely abandoned within two years of the land failing. The nearby forests are all dead and rotting. The nearest source of food is a day's journey; so all food would have to be traded for, but what do they trade with? Seer asked.

I've always liked a good mystery, Mathen thought as he pulled up to the hotel and looked over himself to make sure he was presentable but not overly neat.

Mathen sent his escorts in to make arrangements and stepped down from the wagon to begin tying up the horses. As he finished Seer alerted him to someone coming.

Looks like they have a welcoming committee for you.

Turning around Mathen saw a young boy about 8 or 9 approaching him. The boy was the first smiling face he'd seen so far in town, but it was the type of smile Mathen normally associated with predators moving in of prey. On a boy that young he couldn't decide if it looked cute or disturbing.

"Welcome to Aguares, Sir!" the boy started enthusiastically. "Can I help you with your bags?"

"Thank you but I can manage myself." Mathen answered.

"You're a Necromian aren't you?"

"Yes I am. I'm from Valen, what gave me away?" Mathen asked the boy with a grin.

"Your skin is darker and the top of your ears are a little more pointy. Is it true you live a long time?" the boy asked.

The child fidgeted as he spoke, pacing a little from time to time. Mathen noticed he seemed to slowly fidget closer and closer to him.

"Yes, it's true," Mathen answered. "We have a little elvish blood in us which means we age

Escape through the Sacred Forest

at half the speed of full-blooded humans. I'm 108-years-old."

"What are you doing here in Aguares?"

"I'm a stone cutter. I came about the new quarry."

"Oh, you'll want to talk to Mr. Stoneman across the street," the boy replied.

Mathen looked to the building the boy pointed to which apparently was the moment the boy had waited for. After a quick warning from Seer, and without even looking, Mathen snapped his hand over to his left pocket and grabbed hold of a wrist that was already moving away. Turning around he came face to face with the boy who had both a startled look on his face and Mathen's coin bag in his hand.

It was as Mathen opened his mouth to speak that the vision struck. In all the years that Mathen had possessed Seer, he had had many visions. Hundreds in fact. But the vision he had at this moment was the longest, clearest, and most disturbing vision he had ever had. While the horrors of war, death, and unspeakable crimes he witnessed seemed to go on forever, the vision passed almost instantly in real time as all visions do.

As it ended Mathen found himself still holding the boy's wrist, the coin bag still in hand and a fearful look on his face. The boy... the boy had been the focus of the vision. He had seen glimpses of the boy's terrible future -- or better said the terrible future this boy would create.

Printed in Great Britain
by Amazon